"A sto
ever r
corrosive climax."
Dorothy Hughes on *The Velvet Well*

"Single-minded suspense."
Kirkus Reviews

"Opulently visualized scenes and an
operatic sort of larger-than-life intrigue."
Anthony Boucher,
New York Times Book Review

"Remains a masterpiece of its kind that
combines action, spying, tracking,
mystery, anxiety."
Claude Mesplède on *The Velvet Well*

"Gold Medal's foray into the world of
espionage began in 1950, with its first
fiction release, John Flagg's *The Persian
Cat*."
George Tuttle, "The Gold Medal Boys"

JOHN FLAGG BIBLIOGRAPHY
(1885-1970)

The Persian Cat (1950)
Death and the Naked Lady (1951)
The Lady and the Cheetah (1951)

Hart Muldoon series:
Woman of Cairo (1953)
Dear, Deadly Beloved (1954)
Murder in Monaco (1957)
Death's Lovely Mask (1958)
The Paradise Gun (1961)

As John Gearon

The Velvet Well (1946)

THE PERSIAN CAT
JOHN FLAGG

Black Gat Books • Eureka California

THE PERSIAN CAT

Published by Stark House Press
1315 H Street
Eureka, CA 95501
griffinskye3@sbcglobal.net
www.starkhousepress.com

THE PERSIAN CAT

ISBN: 1-933586-90-7
ISBN-13: 978-1-933586-90-8

Book design by Mark Shepard, shepgraphics.com

First Stark House Press Edition: August 2015
FIRST EDITION

Chapter I

This was a night like any other night, a night with the same needs, a woman, cash and of course, a drink. I had the drink. Sitting on the terrace of the small cafe in the Rue Vaugiard, watching the green Paris night, luminous beneath low hanging clouds, watching the green Paris night and the same old lovers in the Luxembourg gardens, I might as well have been holding aloft a placard reading: FOR SALE TO THE HIGHEST BIDDER, my slogan in a one-man picket line against the world.

I had the drink. It was cognac and good. And there was a girl, four tables away, who seemed at first glance (maybe helped by the green light) not too bad and definitely available whenever I should make up my mind. Inside the cafe someone was fiddling with the radio and after a bit a scratching version of an American song jangled across the terrace. I used to dance with Dorothy to that song and I tried not to hear it, pushing it back into the long-ago, long, long ago back before 1942. But I couldn't get it back far enough; it wouldn't leave me alone. Maybe she was dancing to that maudlin tune tonight in some Grosse Point ballroom or in one of those noisy roadhouses outside Detroit. And I thought of all the other girls like her dancing to the damned tune in New York's Persian Room or the Stork or Morocco—clean-cut, sweet little bitches with their arms wrapped around some guy who had cleaned up on the black-market or got a citation from the government for making several millions producing the stuff we used to do the killing.

I hadn't been back to the States since the army sent me a polite invitation back in '42 and now in '47 I wasted no time on nostalgia. There was nothing I wanted back there. No grey home on Main Street or kids to ask "Daddy, what did you do in the war?" No white haired mother, no proud papa, no nothing. And no job. This was home: a cafe table in Paris or Brussels or Prague or Istanbul or Cairo.

The girl was watching me with professional curiosity. My glass was empty. Something green now, I thought, to go with the night. Maybe shut my eyes over a Pernod and dream of absinthe. I smiled tentatively at the girl and was about to indicate the empty chair at my table when quite suddenly it was no longer empty. A man had got there and he was leaning across the table to grasp my hand.

"Denby!" he said. "M'sieu Gil. It is a miracle!"

It took me a few seconds. Then I said, "Pinel, you old son-of-a-bitch!" But I felt no enthusiasm. After all he had been one of the good men. He brought back some of the things I wanted to forget, the time of bright illusion.

Automatically, by common consent, as though both conforming to an Emily Post primer for a new world, we skipped the "what have you been doing" stuff. I ordered a drink for him and we began talking of other things while I tried to keep the reticence from my voice. We hadn't seen each other since '44, the night we blew up a German troop train on a bridge in the Haut-Marne. He was a big blond ox from Normandy who had been a combat pilot until Weygand folded. His name was Aristide Pinel.

"Are you now living in Paris?" I asked.

He shrugged. "Now and then."

I sensed that he was trying to size me up and I wished to hell he would go. Out of the corner of my eye I watched the girl. She was at a rear table, impassive, dark eyes in a pale face. Pinel did most of the talking. Small talk about a girl we had had, the new show at the Playel, a Sartre opening. After a while I stopped watching the girl and began to listen, not to his words but underneath them. He was after something.

I decided to stop him.

"How much is there in it for me," I asked.

The smile left his face and for an instant there was something hard and bitter in his eyes.

"So?"

"Exactly," I said.

I signalled the waiter. Pinel refused a second drink and when I looked up at him his expression was polite and businesslike.

"Your face," he said. "That is what I meant by 'the miracle.' Maybe..."

"Maybe what?"

He picked up his gloves and stood without offering his hand. "I have friends in the Deuxième," he said. "They mentioned your satisfactory work for them."

"It wasn't much of a job and the pay was good."

"Yes. It has been pleasant. Perhaps sometime soon you will allow me to buy you a drink. Where are you staying?"

I hesitated a moment but finally thought, what the hell, and told him.

He didn't make a note of it. He nodded coolly and said, "Au revoir."

"Goodbye."

He went away into the green night and I sat down again, suddenly angry. The waiter had brought another drink. To hell with that crap, I thought. I turned around. The girl had disappeared. The terrace was deserted now. I sat for a while among the empty tables, wondering why the cognac tasted flat.

I was not altogether surprised when, three days later, my concierge handed me a letter. It was a brief note from a Doctor Julien Caillaux in the Place Vendôme asking me to see him at my earliest convenience. I had a feeling Pinel was there somewhere in the background and my first impulse was to disregard it. But then I figured I had made my position clear to Pinel and decided to go.

Caillaux's office was in one of those Louis XIV buildings opposite the Ritz, and he proved to be a dentist. From the looks of the waiting room and signed photographs on the wall I gathered that he must be one of those big shots who, before the war, polished the choppers of the Duchess of Windsor and half the American colony. I wondered where the photographs had been during the occupation.

The nurse was too young and attractive to be so cold and business-like. She knew my name.

"Your x-rays are ready, Monsieur," she said with a perfectly dead pan.

I looked around at the empty waiting room and grinned. She was not amused. I thought, someone's been seeing too many Hitchcock films, but I played along and said, "Good," in a sepulchral voice and she led me down a long hall and into an operating room where she deposited me firmly on a metal swivel chair and tucked a napkin around my neck.

"If this is a throat-cutting job, make it neat."

Her eyes responded with all the animation of a block of granite. "Dr. Caillaux will be with you directly," she said coolly.

Her uniform crackled with starch as she marched to the door. There was a click and I was left alone in white silence. I lit a cigarette and smoked almost half of it before a man in a white coat came through another door, closed it carefully behind him and stood there examining me as though I were a piece of interesting new machinery. I didn't like it much, but I took time to return the appraisal.

He was a young fifty, tall and military in bearing, a thin aristocratic face, a small scar beneath his left eye. He wore the rosette of the Legion of Honor on his jacket; I wondered whether he wore it to bed.

I handed him the letter. Without averting his steady gaze he tore it up and deposited it in a metal container near the door.

"Pinel was right," he said. "It is quite remarkable."

"I thought Pinel probably had something to do with this, but why all the Black Mask stuff?"

"Comment?"

"The hocus pocus. The Hollywood spy stuff."

"We must be careful," he said shortly.

I didn't get the gimmick. Black market dealings? Hardly, with Pinel in it.

"If I may ask, what is it that is so remarkable?"

"Your face, Monsieur Denby. It resembles someone dead."

The irony in his voice was barely perceptible and before I had a chance to figure out whether a double entendre was intended, he stepped to my side, grabbed a drill and started to work on a realistic looking tooth imbedded in an upper plate sitting on the instrument tray.

"I'm allergic to that noise," I said.

He shrugged apologetically but didn't let up. "My nurse," he explained. "She likes to think I am doing some honest work."

I tried to put my mind on other things and after a bit he stopped the drill. The sound died out with an ugly mutter.

Caillaux offered me a cigarette. "Now then, M. Denby, am I correct in assuming that you are—as the actors say — 'at liberty'?"

"Depends."

"Yes. Quite. Pinel suggested you for this job. I am not in the habit of employing any stray cat from the street. We have made an investigation. Your O.S.S. training, the fact that you have recently completed an important bit of work for the Deuxième Bureau..."

"At a price," I reminded him.

"Ah yes. A price." He gave me a cool, blank stare. I decided not to break the beautiful silence. After a moment he went on. "Once, Monsieur, you were not so interested in 'price.' When you worked with us before."

"Us?"

"The Maquis."

"That was before," I said.

"The fight still goes on."

"Your fight, not mine!"

He shrugged again. For the first time I noticed the faint odor of chloroform in the room; it seemed to come from his clothes.

"Our 'price' is fair enough. But I'm afraid that mere price would not be enough to insure your loyalty. There might be others who could top our price."

"I have a stopping point," I said.

He smiled for the first time.

"Your loyalty then is to the original check?"

"That's one way of putting it," I said it casually enough but I couldn't understand why I was getting riled.

He walked to the far wall and sat in a chair. We were yards apart now.

"This particular job..." he began.

But I interrupted quick, surprised by the violence in my voice. "Price first. Saves time."

"Seven thousand dollars and all expenses."

"That's a starting point," I said. "Now you can talk and I'll tell you whether or not it's my kind of music."

The cool, analytical look again. And something else, very faint and far away. Derision?

"This is not Deuxième business, M. Denby. In fact, it has no official sanction. I am of a group of former resistance officers; we have some unfinished business."

I remembered suddenly the old oath of the Maquis. The oath to bring to justice any individual directly or indirectly responsible for the torturing of a Frenchman during the war.

"Ordinarily," he continued, "we do not find it necessary to employ... er... professional assistance. But this case is rather unusual. The individual involved has powerful protection."

He got up and began to pace back and forth as though he were on the parade ground.

"Only recently," he said, "we have obtained, through investigation of Gestapo files, what we believe to be irrefutable proof that during the war, this person was responsible for the torture and death of three men... one an Englishman and the other two French... but all three patriots. Now then, our purpose is more than mere blood revenge. We believe we have enough evidence to denounce this individual to a French civil court as a murderess. The resulting trial would receive enormous publicity. That is our goal. We believe people must be reminded that all those who once hurt France will some day be punished." He lifted his shoulders ironically. "It is not always a popular point of view these days. It necessitates a certain amount of secret work."

"If you have the evidence, why do you wait? Why do you not denounce this person to the government immediately?"

He sighed. "Our main problem at the moment is to persuade the murderess to step within our jurisdiction. At the moment she is not on French soil."

"She?"

"Exactly. You see, Monsieur, her trial and conviction would set an example for a certain type of female who has meddled too often and with tragic results in the affairs of France. It is time the dangers of boudoir politics be brought home to the public."

"This woman was a salon politician?"

"No. As a matter of fact, she is not even French. But she is the type of irresponsible parasitic female who climbs to her pinnacle in a Rolls Royce over the bodies of the betrayed."

"This isn't a kidnapping deal?"

"Perhaps. But we believe there are other methods you might employ with success."

"For instance."

"Pinel was struck immediately with your resemblance to the murdered man. The man who was once her husband and for whom, curiously enough, she possessed a sentimental attachment."

"You mean *I'm* to employ boudoir tactics?"

He smiled. "Touché. But Pinel informs me it is not the least of your attributes."

"Only a Frenchman would have thought of this," I said.

"Perhaps, Monsieur, only a Frenchman would *admit* to having thought of it."

"It doesn't make sense," I said. "You think I can... er... ingratiate myself with this modern Lucrezia Borgia because of my resemblance to her former husband. You say she had a sentimental attachment to him. Then why did she put him out of the way?"

"We believe she realized he was dangerous to her ambitions. A weakness which must be disposed of. He offered her nothing in comparison to the man whose mistress she became..."

"Who is she?"

"Her name is Claire Fayne."

It struck a faint bell.

"Her husband was Reginald Fayne, a British agent who worked with our people in the resistance. She was interned at Vichy and her house was used as... what we believed to be... a safe base of operations. It is our contention that she betrayed us, to get rid of her husband in order to enjoy the protection and wealth of Edmund Marlan."

"Marlan!"

I reached for a cigarette. There was a silence as I lighted it. I tried to conceal my inner excitement. At least there wouldn't be a dull moment in a deal that involved Marlan. He was one of the most inscrutable and mysterious figures in the international scene. His power reached into large business corporations in France, England, Sweden, the States and

points east, west, south and north. Although the second
world war had been merely an interlude in his international
chess game—a game that had included visits to Goering's
shooting lodge, dinners with Petain, weekends with Ciano,
business appointments in Detroit and New York and resi-
dences in Nassau, Mexico City, Paris and London—the al-
lied governments had failed to prove any open act of collaboration with the enemy. And perhaps the final judgment
had been correct (at least technically). From what I had heard
about the guy, he had collaborated with no one but Marlan.

Finally I said, "How did Mrs. Fayne dispose of her husband?"

"She betrayed him to the Millace, the Vichy secret police.
Inadvertently she also betrayed two more of our men. One
of whom was my brother-in-law. The three men were tortured to death. Mrs. Fayne was not molested. In fact she
joined Marlan in Lisbon the following week."

I blew smoke up into the white room trying to analyze the
sensation of disgust the name Marlan induced in me. After
all, had I not become a small time Marlan, in my own manner? Marlan had merely arrived where I was now, years before.

"You are positive that this woman was the one who betrayed her husband to the Millace?"

Caillaux smiled coldly. "What do you think? She was not
arrested herself? She was allowed to leave France to join
Marlan?"

"Circumstantial," I said.

"Besides, there are many other things. Servants oven heard
them quarreling very frequently near the end. The quarrels
were on one subject: an effort on her part to persuade her
husband to desert his duties and to join up with Marlan in
Lisbon. Apparently she had some hope of making him not
only a traitor but a willing cuckold. He refused. She took the
easy way out. It is quite obvious."

I thought so too. I crushed out the cigarette in a porcelain bowl beside the chair.

"Where are they now, Marlan and the girl? Over what borders am I to lead her?"

"First, Monsieur, I must know whether or not you are willing to take on the assignment?"

"With Marlan involved, my price goes up. It's ten thousand and expenses."

Like most Frenchmen he was a horse-trader from way back. We finally settled for eight thousand. I left him in the white room and went out through the office. The nurse nodded goodbye and even managed an automatic smile. But her eyes were cold as stone.

Chapter 2

The following day I lunched at Maria's near the Dome. The appointment was for three p.m. at a number on the Boulevard Raspiel within easy walking distance of the restaurant. I couldn't understand my inner feeling of reluctance. A deal like this one certainly offered plenty of excitement along with a good hunk of cash. Even Maria's omelette aux fines herbes and, for these days, a surprisingly good bottle of Chablis, didn't assuage the inexplicable nagging worry in the back of my mind. The morning had seen me in the morgue of the *Paris Herald* doing some homework on Edmund Marlan. But the latest news report on him, four months old, placed him at his villa near Mexico City and none of the boys around the office seemed to know his present whereabouts.

Over my coffee, I glanced casually through the Paris Herald. I felt a sudden shock as I noticed a name in the social notes. Quickly, unbelieving, I read the item:

"Mr. and Mrs. Wilson Bond, who have been
at the Ritz for the past two weeks, left last night
by plane for Cairo where Mr. Wilson will personally supervise the opening of the Egyptian
branch of Bond Motors."

Dorothy! Dorothy Wilson Bond, greeted with proper def-
erence by headwaiters, traveling de luxe in a starving world,
seeing the decay of Europe from the safety of the Ritz. For
the past two weeks she had been here in the same city, near
enough to reach by lifting a telephone receiver. Vividly, a
little scene took place in my mind, a monologue natural to
Dorothy. "Darling, how divine... now don't be so dull...
worships the ground I walk on... and so sweet... and so lib-
eral... out all afternoon on business... and if you'll come,
darling, so much to talk about, Gil darling..."

Near enough to paste in the jaw!

I shut her from my mind, locked her out, tried to ignore
the sudden feeling of weariness and indifference. The restaurant was deserted now except for Maria behind her high
desk, a sleepy waiter and an incredibly genteel middle-aged
woman who lunched alone at a corner table, darting at her
food with furtive, bird-like gestures.

I looked at my watch. Still three quarters of an hour to go.
I paid my bill, avoided a tête a tête with Maria, retrieved my
suitcase and walked out into the spring sun. For Paris, the
street scene was peculiarly dull and lethargic. I wandered
down to the river and, placing my bag on the pavement,
leaned against the parapet. The sky was washed clean of
clouds and the old stone of the buildings on the Île de la Cité
seemed etched into the clear air. A slim little river boat darted
upstream, collapsing its smoke stack beneath the bridge with
a sort of comic smugness. The towers of Notre Dame rose
over the ancient house-tops, the sounds of the city seemed
muffled and dreamlike.

I thought, there's still time to turn back.

I stared down into the slow-moving water, wondering at my uneasiness. There was something. Something. Nothing mystical, of course, no gypsy's premonition. But something. Maybe it was because my luck had held out for so long, now.

The eddies and currents of the river seemed suddenly to be part of an inexorable whole, moving forward relentlessly to some terrifying future. And as I stood there, half somnolent, I suddenly had a sharp, almost overwhelming sense of nostalgia. Not for people but for places. A white house, maybe, near a village square, the green rolling hills of Connecticut. Some place with peace in it.

And then I thought, Jesus, I must be getting old.

I picked up my bag and walked swiftly towards the Boulevard Raspiel.

A woman opened the door of apartment twenty-two. She was short and slim with dark, curly hair clustered about the face of a mischievous choir boy. She wore a thin blouse unbuttoned an inch below respectability, and slacks. In the instant I stood on the threshold she gave me a complete once-over. She smiled and right away I liked her. She stepped aside (no word passed between us) and I walked past her into one of those depressing petit bourgeois living rooms where dark wallpaper was spattered with unlikely roses and there was grim, uncomfortable furniture mixed up with a lot of tawdry bric-a-brac. Pinel was sitting on a horse-hair sofa.

"Put your bag in there," he said, indicating a door behind him. He had some papers before him on a low coffee table, and he turned back to them as I crossed to the door. The other room was a small bedroom with an enormous but uncomfortable looking bed, an imitation marble fireplace, a commode on which stood a basin and pitcher. I put my bag down and returned to the living room. The girl was sprawled across an armchair with her legs over the arms, dropping cigarette ashes on the faded carpet.

"This is Gaby Duval," Pinel said shortly. "She'll work with you."

"That sounds like fun," I said. Gaby smiled.

"Sit down, Denby."

I sat opposite him. He looked up from the papers. His eyes were not exactly unfriendly but they could not have been described as overflowing with warmth.

"You may come back later, Gaby," he said. The girl pouted goodnaturedly, gave me a ravishing smile, and hatless and coatless left the apartment.

"Does that come with the apartment?" I asked Pinel.

He raised his eyebrows. "If you do not find her to your taste..."

"She looks all right to me. I suppose her instructions are not to let me out of her sight."

He looked impassive. "There is too much money floating around the streets. It is better that you stay here in Gaby's apartment until you are ready to depart from the country."

"I've had worse jailors," I said.

"We must not waste time," Pinel said sharply. "We have much preparatory work to do."

I spent most of the afternoon boning up on the personal histories of Claire Fayne and her husband Reginald. The gimmick was that by the time I approached Claire Fayne I would be letter-perfect in the role of an old friend of her husband. It seems that although I had never met Claire I had been a close friend of Reginald, close enough to know the more intimate details of their relationship. Where and how Pinel and Company had got hold of these little details was a mystery understood perhaps only by another Frenchman. About five o'clock he began drilling me.

"Summer, 1938?"

"Monte Carlo. The business about the lobsters."

"Where did they stay?"

"Antibes."

"The hotel! Quick! The hotel!"

"Calm yourself. The Hôtel de Cap, of course."

"Oxford, 1934?"

"I met Reginald. I was a Rhodes scholar, and he was up for his last term. Later we met when he visited New York."

"Year. The year."

"Hold on a minute..."

"The year!" He shouted, "Be more positive!"

"Even Gielgud couldn't be letter perfect in such a short time."

Exasperated, he began to drum the details into my head and then the drilling recommenced. When I would slip up he would press his fists to the side of his head and glare at me and my grin would only drive him into a fresh paroxysm of rage.

"Imbecile! This is no game. When did you next meet up with Fayne?"

"Not until the war years. In France when we were both working for the resistance. First at Lyon, and later right here in Paris. It was during this period that he talked about his wife, describing her in such extravagant terms that I vowed to look her up after the shooting was over."

"What was his nickname for her?"

"Famous. God knows why, but that was it."

"You see. 'God knows why,' he says! What God is doubtful about, you must be certain of. 'Famous' he called her, because it is the Latin for Claire. He used it in moments of intimacy and endearment."

"Some guy, this Fayne, spouting Latin under the sheet!"

"Later some of their crowd picked it up."

"Yeah, yeah."

A key grated in the lock and Gaby came in bearing packages. She went to a screen in the corner and disappeared behind it and soon there was the sound of pots and pans. Pinel leaned back and lit a cigarette.

"That's all for today. I'll be here at nine tomorrow morning. In the meantime you might study these tonight." He handed me a sheaf of closely typed pages.

Gaby came from behind the screen with a tray holding a bottle and three glasses. Pinel looked from the bottle to me and I saw the color rising to his face.

"I must go," he said painfully.

"Perhaps tomorrow you'll drink with me," I said.

"Yes... yes. Perhaps tomorrow."

Gaby went out into the hall with him and I heard them talking together in low voices. By the time she came back I was well into the first glass of wine.

"It will be nice, fixing your dinner," she said.

"I bet you tell that to all the boys."

For a moment she looked puzzled, then she said, "No. It is not necessary, really. I tell it to you because I mean it."

The dinner was all right. I fed my stomach and I fed my eyes. Gaby kept her lids lowered toward her plate, except now and then when she asked me if I wanted more tea or more of the thick black bread. She wasn't being coy, but the lack of design on her part had the opposite effect on me. The more I ate, the hungrier I became.

When she was doing the dishes, I got impatient. The room was in velvet gloom now. She washed saucers with a slow rotary motion of the wrist. She stood almost too straight, so that her back curved inward at the waist. Her ankles were stolid; not thick, but stolid. You looked at them and thought of peasant Poles and peasant Germans and peasant Chinese. You thought of barns and hayricks and compost and big white mugs of wine with dinner. You thought of miles-deep feather mattresses and room to roll and bedchambers with large red roses painted on the side.

I got up from the couch. I grabbed her around the waist

and opened my mouth and kissed her ear. She dropped something. I didn't hear it break. She tried to squirm away. There was no fright. The time was not of her choosing, that was all. I pulled her to the couch. Softly, as one whispers in church, she kept saying "No, no, no." She didn't say stop. She said no. I started to unbutton the blouse but I had too many working fingers. It was no time for gentility so I took the collar in two hands and pulled. The little buttons danced brightly in the dusk.

Later, much later that evening, she turned on the pillow and said, "It is good to be alive, Gil. When you don't expect anything, life can be... surprising. Now just for a little time I'll pretend it is only you and me and never will there be another."

"Let's not be sentimental," I said.

During the next few days I came almost to hate Pinel. He was relentless. But by the end of the week I nearly believed I had known Reginald Fayne as a close friend. At night the fictitious friendship took on reality in my dreams. Dreamwise, I would sit at a cafe table joking with him, laughing over evenings when we had come down from Oxford to do London, and the weekends with his aristocratic, impoverished family at the county seat in Sussex.

But for some reason, when I dreamed of Claire Fayne, she was always one of those slim, cold-faced blondes with light blue eyes reflecting ice. Thus it came as a complete surprise to me when one day, late in the week, Pinel handed me a photograph of her cut out of a fashionable London magazine. The photograph, dated 1939, was taken in the Royal enclosure at Ascot. It revealed a dark-haired woman with a magnificent figure. She was unsmiling and aloof but the expression in her eyes suggested some secret sadness rather than coldness. Beautifully gowned, more aristocratic looking than the titled women in the picture with her, she was looking directly into the camera and as I stared into her eyes I again felt that odd sensation of uneasiness and foreboding I had felt the afternoon beside the river.

I looked up from the photograph to find Pinel watching me curiously.

"Charming, eh?" he said harshly. "Even I, feeling as I do, experience the warming of the blood when I think of her. Quelle chic... what made her that way!"

Gaby spoke. "It takes a woman to deal with a bitch like that!" She was tense and angry. Also, she was watching me.

"Perhaps she will be too much for you, Denby?"

"I know the type," I said with more ease than I felt. "The whore dressed by Molyneux. They used to come a dime a dozen wherever one found the 'chic' set. I know how to handle the type."

"Oh yes," Gaby said. "He'll handle her all right, no fear of that!"

Pinel looked at Gaby in surprise. Then he turned to me with a raised eyebrow and I saw for the first time a gleam of humor in his eyes.

"Shut up," I said to Gaby.

She slammed out of the room.

"Congratulations. You are a fast worker," Pinel said. "Only the same methods may not be successful on a woman of Mrs. Fayne's experience."

"Never mind that. What's her background?"

"We know she was born in Texas..."

"Texas! Where?"

"Dallas."

"Good Lord. I was born thirty miles from Dallas."

"I know. That should help. However, we have not been able to dig up very much about her early life. The first we see her is when she arrives in London in '38 as Marlan's social secretary. Apparently he picked her up in the States. Whether she was his mistress at that time, we can only guess. It was not generally considered so. However, he did take her about socially. That is how she came to meet Reginald Fayne. They were married in December of '38. Marlan invited them to spend their honeymoon on his yacht, but they went to Antibes instead..."

There was a knock on the door and Pinel opened it to admit Caillaux. I had not seen him since the day in his office in the Place Vendôme. He was brisk and businesslike.

"How is it developing?" he asked Pinel.

Pinel shrugged. "He has his facts straight. He is too sure of himself."

"Ah?" Caillaux came and sat opposite me, leaning forward earnestly. "Now, M. Denby, you must not make the mistake of underrating the opposition. This is not a simple job. We would not have called on you if it were. It requires finesse, a quick mind, a certain understanding of the mental processes of the persons involved—and, perhaps, an adeptness with firearms."

I nodded, said nothing, lit a cigarette.

"Claire Fayne is a clever and unscrupulous woman. However, you are not a callow youth and certainly the tricks of the boudoir are well known to you."

"I've been around, if that's what you mean, and with women like this one."

"Good. Now then..." he leaned back and regarded me as through half-closed eyes. "Edmund Marlan is a different story. He is a highly complex, completely corrupt and extremely dangerous man. In fact, I know of few men alive in the world who are as dangerous. He has tremendous power, financially and in high political places. Those who have tried to interfere with him before have met with disaster. And I mean disaster in the most complete sense of the word. Claire Fayne is his property. He has some nasty individuals to do his dirty work."

"Sounds like Al Capone."

"A not dissimilar type. Capone with window dressing, let

us say. A man with no loyalties except to his own peculiar needs and to power."

"Where is this game of tag due to take place?"

"Teheran."

I straightened up and stubbed out my cigarette.

"Marlan was close to the late Shah. I guess you can guess what his interest is, in Iran."

"What everybody's interest is. Oil."

"Exactly. He lives there like a Prince of India. Mrs. Fayne lives accordingly. You must work on her without arousing his suspicions. Your job is to persuade her to enter French territory. Perhaps Algiers. Our people will take over from there."

"This has possibilities," I said. "Possibilities of sudden death."

"Quite."

He reached into his overcoat, took out a small package and began to unwrap it.

"Pinel and Gaby will be in Teheran. Also some others of our people. We will evolve a system of communication."

"I hope they are there to work with me, not to watch me?"

"That's up to you, monsieur," he said coldly.

As he talked he unwrapped the package to reveal a small china cat about seven inches tall. It was a cheap ornament, one of the thousands made in the souks of Iran. It had a half human face and its stylized red spots were dotted with gold.

"Regardez," he said.

I did so without much interest.

"It looks like any other, does it not?"

"Yes."

"But it has a special meaning for you, monsieur. You see the red dots. They have a peculiar pattern. The object is used by a secret society in Iran to identify its members. I will show you how to use it to identify yourself but you are not to employ it except as a last resort." He chuckled. "We will

call this mission 'Operation Cat.' A double entendre, hein?
The woman and the secret patriots."

I stifled an impulse to laugh. I sensed that Caillaux took
almost an adolescent's pleasure in the lurid atmosphere of
intrigue he managed to sustain. I took the cat from him but
decided that the only help I could ever expect from it would
be from a handful of moth eaten Arabs. I couldn't see why
the job demanded so much conspiratorial secrecy. Mrs. Fayne
had no way of knowing I was headed her way. She was a
smart dish, but it would be fun to trip her up.

Pinel called Gaby from the bedroom. She came out still
looking sullen.

"You will be prepared to leave, tonight, Gaby. Pick up
your papers at my place at eight. Take only one small bag.
Your plane leaves Orly at eleven."

She nodded and turned back to the bedroom.

Caillaux stood and held out his hand. "Good luck," he
said.

I shook hands and thanked him. Pinel stayed behind to
give me some more of the business just to make sure. He
seemed satisfied. Before he left he said, "You will be ready
to leave on Thursday morning. I will explain your 'front' to
you tomorrow."

When he had gone I stood for a moment staring at the
china cat on the table. Outside there were the sudden chimes
of church bells in the early evening air. Gaby appeared in
the doorway carrying a small bag.

She smiled wryly. "Forgive me, Gil. I have no right to be
jealous."

I went to her, took the bag from her hand, and placed it on
the floor.

After a bit, I asked, "You're a sweet kid, Gaby, how did
you happen to get into this business?"

She looked at me in surprise. "This business? It is all I
know. All I care for, really. I was fourteen when the war be-

gan. I was with the Maquis in the Vosges Mountains. I go on fighting in my way, as long as I am useful."

She said it quite simply as though it was incredible to think of another way of life. The daydreams of the average American girl of her age had no place in her life. She was looking up into my face with a sudden, rueful intensity.

"I want to believe that you are good, Gil. I guess I love you very much. But if I should find out you are not good..."

She didn't have to finish. I kissed her tenderly.

"Until Teheran, cherie."

At the door she turned. "Gil," she said seriously. "I know more than they. Pinel and Caillaux. About you, I mean. A woman knows those things. You must stop being a boy. I love the man in you, Gil."

My laugh sounded hollow.

"No," she said gently. "Listen. A woman hurt you, Gil. A woman like the one in that picture. You blame her for everything, don't you?"

"A woman?" I said. "There isn't a woman alive who could hurt me."

"Liar," she said.

She was gone before I realized it. I listened to the sound of her footsteps on the uncarpeted stairs. A small sound, but firm and sure of its destination. I walked slowly to the china cat and picked up the photograph beside it. The face blurred into the face of Dorothy. Dorothy so lovely and cynical and gay and full of promises. Dorothy married to a war-profiteer, queening it over a mansion at Grosse Pointe, doing a "Grand Tour" as though there had never been a war.

Claire Fayne smiled back at me. I began to hate her the way I had been hating Dorothy for a long time.

Chapter 3

An Air-France plane deposited me in Cairo at three o'clock on Friday afternoon. My train for Port Said was not scheduled to leave until six. I checked my bags at the station and walked the few blocks to Shepherd's where I found a table far back in the corner of the terrace and ordered something cool to drink. The effendis and the Europeans sat about in wicker chairs oblivious to the constant stream of poverty that trickled past in the street below. Through the great Moorish arch of the hotel entrance wandered smartly dressed women and well fed men, constantly arriving and departing in expensive limousines. I knew I should not be here. The chances of running into Dorothy were too great. She would be staying either here or at Mena House and all Cairo gathered for tea on the terrace of Shepherd's. At least "all Cairo" that would be her Cairo.

After three drinks, and just as I was preparing to go, she came out through the arch, cool and smart in a silk print frock and an enormous black straw hat. She was accompanied by two men, one middle aged, stocky and red-faced, wearing spotless whites, the other a sleek dark young man who looked Italian, but was dressed as an Englishman in the traditional tweed coat and grey flannels. Dorothy didn't see me. She was too intent in smiling up into the face of the young man. Even at this distance I knew that smile. She might as well have been in his arms. I figured the poor dope in whites was Bond. For a moment I felt almost sorry for him.

Seeing her like this after all this time changed nothing. All the old feelings were smothered in hatred. I sat there still and watching, one hand on the bill, the other on my empty glass, waiting until they had passed across the terrace, down the steps and into a waiting limousine. The car drew away from the curb. The last I saw of her was the enormous black hat hiding her face from the man she had married.

There but for the grace of God, I thought. I put a bill on the table, left the terrace and walked back to the station wondering whether it was the heat or the gin that made me feel so light and vague. The feeling persisted until the train was well out of the city. Only when I dozed did memory drag up out of the unconsciousness what I had resolutely shut out of my waking life. Dorothy, insistent and passionate on the New York hotel bed the night before I sailed, saying, "No one else ever. Only you, if I have to wait till there's no fun in it any more." I shook myself awake, tried a magazine, gave up and concerned myself with the panorama out the window.

The de luxe car in which I travelled was a paradox, a gilded atom from the western world piercing deeper and deeper into the world of the Arab. The deserts and the oasis villages. Veiled women on donkeys beside the tracks, camels rocking across a red sunset. The ancient water wheels beside the wells. And the poverty.

Port Said, as always, where the worst of Moslem civilization met the worst of western civilization, was a madhouse of screaming vendors, pimps, whores, horse-traders from many nations, frigid middle-aged British women under parasols apparently unaware that the Empire was crumbling into history. The city of deals in back rooms. The city where everything from love to murder could be had for a price. Beneath my hotel window an Arab orchestra screeched into the hot, garishly lighted night till dawn.

I mounted the gangplank of an evil looking Turkish tramp steamer shortly after sunrise for the slow voyage to Abadan. My fellow passengers were two: a Roumanian of uncertain age who would have delighted Caillaux with his cat-like silence about his prospective business in Iran; a nervous talkative young Frenchman who claimed he represented an

American drug company and was about to introduce vitamin neurosis to the Iranians but whom I immediately spotted as a Caillaux plant. I had a little fun for a few hours, misleading him as much as possible, but after a while the heat got the better of me and I retired to the uncertain privacy of my cabin for the remainder of our voyage. As I suspected, I lost my Frenchman at Abadan and heard neither of him nor of his vitamins again.

Those who were in the Persian Gulf Command during the war have done their share to publicize the temperature of the hellhole called Abadan, but the written word simply cannot convey the unspeakable heat of the city. My whites were soaked through an hour after breakfast and I felt like a couple of lost weekends. But I had a break in one direction. Inconsistently enough, Caillaux had directed that I travel to the capitol by plane rather than the army built railroad. The movement of the plane (an ancient KLM model) through the upper air gave me the illusion, at least, of escape from the heat. I had the misfortune to sit next to a rarity, a talkative Englishman, a naval attaché who exhibited a peculiarly un-British tendency to act as my personal guide to the relief map below us. Lacking the professional invention of a spieler on a Chinatown bus, his monologue soon became strangely monotonous and after the eleventh reference to romantic caravans and the personal idiosyncrasies of the camel, I began to doze. But when I heard the words "Masjid-i-Sulaiman," I woke up and looked below. Directly ahead was a metallic spotch on the landscape, Anglo-Persian's best drillings. It looked like a hunk of home to me. But at the same time it looked somehow wrong, blatant and arrogant and as out of place as an American Eagle woven into a Persian rug.

"We call it the Admiralty," the Britisher was saying proudly. "Stop its flow and His Majesty's Navy suffers."

It took only a moment to leave behind the scar on the wide map, but I thought about it the rest of the way to Teheran. I thought of the blotch of oil spreading its scum slowly across other maps and the other navies and airforces and the other attachés, official and otherwise, who were drawn to the derricks like steel to a magnet. And I thought of Marlan.

From desert to steppes to low dusty-looking hills, and suddenly we began spiralling down towards a city. Teheran rose to meet us like an illustration from *Thousand and One Nights*, slightly faded, scrawled upon by a western schoolboy with his own little ideas of "improvements." It was a walled city with twelve gates, sprawled on a broad plain of gravel that seemed to spill down from the mountains. Narrow snakes of streets and broad tree-lined boulevards. Acres of white mud-houses broken by gems of oriental splendor. And, here and there, like cancerous growths, clusters of European houses and buildings.

The British naval attaché regretted he would go north in the morning and that in all probability our paths would never cross again. I felt almost guilty for not sharing his regret. The customs inspection was perfunctory. The Iranian douanier went through my bags in a bored, openly cynical manner, disregarding the carton of cigarettes as though he had suddenly gone blind. But when he came to the Persian Cat his manner changed slightly. He looked up at me with guarded alertness and after a moment he held his thumb over the left eye of the cat and placed his index finger on the red gold spot on the top of the head.

"I see," he said, smiling blandly, "that you have the interest in the Persian art?"

Baby, I thought, Caillaux would love you. But I disregarded the signal and played dumb. "Picked it up in a bazaar at Abadan," I said, "my sister's kid might like it."

He looked uncertain for a moment, then shrugged, and dropped the cat back into my bag with a gesture of utter indifference. But as I walked out through the barrier I was aware of him standing there behind me, watching.

I tossed my bag into a droshky, the local version of the yel-low-cab, and told the driver to take me to the Hôtel Provençal. In a leisurely manner we made our way through narrow streets and into the wide Boulevard des Ambas-sadeurs, lined on both sides by comparatively imposing lega-tion buildings. The poplar trees along the way looked dusty and half dead. Just off one of the dusty squares we came to a stop before a top-heavy, ill-kept building decorated with useless grilled balconies and large gold letters across the sec-ond floor balcony informing the world and his brother that this was the Hôtel Provençal. A tired old Arab took my bag without enthusiasm as I haggled with the driver. We had just arrived at a compromise (involving only minor highway robbery) when I saw Gaby. She was standing in front of a French modiste's shop next to the hotel. She was looking into the window but I caught her eye in the reflection of the plate glass. She gave no sign of recognition.

As I turned from the droshky she began to move along the pavement casually, so that our paths met in front of the hotel entrance.

"Pardon, Madame," I said, lifting my hat. She slid the note deftly into my hand, nodded coolly and passed on. For a moment I watched her pert little behind wagging down the street. I walked into the dim hotel lobby. There were wilted potted palms, a tiled floor like a bathroom, an ancient electric fan revolving slowly in the ceiling, a door to the left of the desk with a sign over it reading "American Bar," wicker chairs, two or three dilapidated plush sofas, a French-man behind the desk, a man in whites who sat in one of the wicker chairs with a newspaper between me and his face.

I registered, stepped behind the open grillwork of the ele-vator cage and caught the man in whites bringing up his newspaper just a moment too late. I knew he had been watch-ing me. The machine clanged upward and, amid tortured rattlings, in a few moments I was in my room, a room that showed not only the neglect of the war years but all the stress and strain of too many visits by lusty members of the Persian Gulf Command on leave. After a shower I wrapped a towel around my middle and glanced through the newspaper I had picked up in the lobby. The stream of air from the electric fan was warm. Outside the window the city looked hot and tired, the distant hills were brown.

Gaby's note had read, "J. J. Siraud, 3 Rue Revjed, 5 o'-clock." It was now only two in the afternoon.

I glanced through the social notes of the paper hoping to find some mention of either Marlan or Claire Fayne. There was nothing. The notes were sad little items, simliar in tone to those in a small town American paper, embellished now and then by a title, suggesting a limited group of Europeans forced to gaze upon the same faces, the same activities, the same dream of a white man's superior civilization among the savages. The front page was agitated over what was termed "Communist uprisings in the north," the tone of which was somewhat mitigated by a reference in another story to the "great heart" of "our honorable neighbor to the north." I thought of all the attachés of the various consulates tossing in their afternoon siestas and all the headaches. Same old world, I thought, looking out at the weary, dust-laden city, only more so. Same old stinking rat-race. I joined the attachés and others in a siesta. Or tried to. Beneath the torn mosquito netting, Dorothy taunted me until I expelled her finally from my bed with the epithet which had become synonymous in my mind with her name.

And in my dream, after Dorothy, there was Gaby, simple and direct, wearing her heart on her sleeve and an inexplicable feeling of guilt as though I were about to deflower a fourteen year old virgin and her saying, "I am fourteen and they killed my father and my brother, so it's all right." And suddenly she was no longer there and I called for Dorothy, called for her with that word, but the door opened and a woman from a photograph was there walking in from the hall where a group from the Royal Enclosure waited, smiling lewdly. And suddenly the face, as she came towards me, dissolved into Jim McBride's, half destroyed the way it had been the minute before he died in that ditch beside the railroad tracks at Dijon. And Jim was saying, "she did it to me in Vichy."

I woke up in a cold sweat and dozed again, dreaming that my life was a bad dream; woke this time for good and tried to dispel the sickening sensation in my stomach by saying, "For Christ's sake, so what!"

I went down to the "American Bar" and had a shot of Burke's. The man in whites who had been sitting behind the newspaper when I first entered the hotel wandered in. I knew immediately that he was British. But he had none of the fresh innocence of the companion of the plane; he had a grey, guarded look, was thin in an ill manner, with sandy dry-looking hair and very pale blue eyes. I finished my drink quickly before he could sidle up to me at the bar, and walked past him towards the lobby. He gave me a tired smile.

"Mr. Peters been in, Fares?" he asked the barman.

"No sir."

"In that case I'll be back later."

Who are you fooling, baby, I thought, aware that he was following me towards the hotel entrance. I waited down the street after leaving the lobby. Sure enough, he came out, glanced in my direction, met my eyes, hesitated, shrugged and returned once more to the hotel. I took no chances. Affecting the casual tourist, I used the narrow back streets and after inquiring for the Rue Revjed from a police officer finally entered the broad square of the Maidan Tupkhaneh, near the gardens of the Gulistan Palace, the home of the Peacock Throne. The place swarmed with desert tribesmen rubbing elbows with Europeanized Iranians on the pavements and at the coffee tables. Most of the women wore chadars and they appeared to be so many listless blackbirds.

I circled aimlessly through the crowd, making sure my British friend was not behind me, before I finally entered the Rue Revjed. Number Three was a shabby office building. Inside the street door I found a directory and walked up a flight of wide wooden stairs to a gloomy hall. Number twenty-seven was at the end of the hall in the rear of the building. Gold lettering on the door read: "J. J. Siraud, Les Tapis Persiens, et les Objets Iraniens—Londres, Paris, Teheran." Inside the place was a rug museum and a maze of tables and cabinets, exhibiting ancient Persian knick-knacks. A sloe-eyed Iranian girl got up from a roll top desk and asked my business.

"Mr. Siraud in?"

"The name, please, and the nature of the business?"

"Denby, New York. He'll know."

"Denbee? Un moment." She went back among the rugs towards a small green baize door and almost immediately Gaby came out.

"My uncle has gone to Cairo," she said in a businesslike voice, "perhaps I can help you."

"Yes," I said, "you could."

She frowned. I liked the new dress she wore. As usual, her breasts were a fraction of an inch away from indecent exposure.

In French, she told the Iranian girl to get herself some coffee and that she would listen for the telephone. The girl didn't seem much interested but picked up a beret from the roll top desk and went out. I followed Gaby quickly into a small office behind the baize door. She shut the door, leaned back against it and shut her eyes. Her lips were frantic against mine. Somehow we got to the divan in the corner.

"A fine way to conduct business," she said.

The smoke from our cigarettes was hanging in a low cloud in the dead air. She was perched now on the desk, looking for all the world as though she had just stepped out of a cool shower.

"Isn't it," I said.

"Yes."

We laughed. Then she got serious.

"The woman is giving a reception tomorrow night in her villa. It is wise that you be there."

"With what for an invitation?"

"We could have arranged one of course, but it is not so good that you should be sponsored by anyone we know. I think perhaps you will have to rely on your charm and persuasion. I am of the impression that you Americans call this a crashing of the gates."

"I should think that would make me as welcome as a leper in the Stork Club."

"Perhaps. But considering you are supposed to have been one of the friends of the husband, I doubt she would dare to show it. Anyway, once you get in," her voice became brittle, "I have no doubt you will find a way to ingratiate yourself."

"You should know!"

"Don't be vulgar!"

"Look here, Gaby," I began.

She slid off the desk, standing very straight before me. "I don't know what has got into me," she said. "I am never like this before. Not about anyone. I do not believe I like it."

"There are other Gaby's I like better," I admitted. I felt uneasy.

"Gil?"

"Well, cherie?"

She was looking into my eyes with an intensity that only increased my uneasiness.

"You are going to do the right thing."

"I don't know what you mean by 'right.' If you mean the job..."

"You know what I mean! Dammit, you know!"

"If you mean, am I going to sell out to anyone else, the answer is no."

She was silent for a moment. "Gil?"

I moved restlessly. "Yes?"

"Is there, I mean do you think after, for you and me..."

I managed to get off the couch and moved to the window and stood there with my back to her, feeling suddenly angry.

"Listen, Gaby. I don't want to be a heel. I'm not the guy they sing about in the songs. There's no hearth rugs or babies or Sunday church in my picture. There's no eternity. And there aren't any promises."

She was very quiet. Again the odd feeling of guilt I had experienced in the dream returned. I imagined a fourteen year old kid standing there in the sultry room behind me. The silence became unendurable and I turned with an impatient word on my lips. But when I saw her face I stopped. She was smiling. A small smile but a smile nevertheless.

"All right, Gil," she said. "I was just wondering. Don't worry. It's all right that way."

I went to her, managing only with great effort not to say the things I might later regret and had her in my arms again when the door suddenly opened and Pinel was there.

Without a flicker of embarrassment, he said, "Fools!"

We fell apart.

He shut the door behind him and sat at the desk. "Gaby has probably explained to you," he said, not without irony, "that here she is the niece of M. Siraud. She has arrived only last week from her home in Bordeaux to help her uncle in his business."

"She explained," I lied. Gaby grinned.

"I'm glad that you have found some time for business."

"Yes, thank you. We had time."

"Despite the fact that I am a Frenchman, Denby, I can have sympathy with certain of your activities only if they are a rehearsal for what is to come."

I clicked my heels in an exaggerated manner. "Oui, mon capitaine."

"Now then, have you anything to report?"

"Yes. The British Overseas plane to Cairo made certain peculiar deviations from its course over the Greek islands, the food aboard the Turkish tub was abominable, there was a Frenchman aboard whom I suspect of being in league with the Arab *Congress...*"

"Enough!" Pinel threw down his pencil angrily. "This so called humor is nothing but an American form of exhibitionism. I have not the time to..."

"All right. There's a seedy looking limey at the Provençal who has taken it on himself to tail me."

Gaby and Pinel exchanged a quick glance.

"Describe him."

I did so. Pinel looked slightly worried.

"This town is a hotbed of intrigue and power politics and the more unsavory aspects of big business. Any newcomer is suspect. This Englishman is probably employed by one of these groups or countries. Maybe by more than one. Remember you are to imply that you are in the employ of an American department store. You are here to buy rugs. The Englishman may only be curious as to your, uh, racket. But be careful."

"All the quaint charm of the near east," I said.

"Gil," Gaby said, "please do not be reckless. You don't know this city."

Pinel leaned back and lit a cigarette. "Last night, a riot among the Khorramshar oil workers left three men dead and many broken heads. A powerful Arab leader, friendly to the British, was clubbed and beheaded in the street."

"What's that got to do with us?"

"It is vital that you are not mistaken for a political agent. Otherwise we would have the watchdogs of several nations interfering with our plans. If you have the chance to engage the Englishman at the Provençal in conversation be sure and convince him that your work is for the American department store."

Gaby was closing the shutters against the falling sun. Suddenly she froze, with a shutter half closed.

"Gil, come here."

I peered over her shoulder. She nodded in the direction of the coffee house across the street. There under the awning sat a man in whites.

"Is that him?"

"Yes. Goddamn it, I thought I'd shaken the bastard."

Pinel joined us, pushing me roughly aside. After a moment he said, "Close the shutter, Gaby."

She obeyed. The room was plunged into a damp gloom. Pinel returned to the desk. He didn't look directly at me. "That man, his name is Berkeley," he said. "Ostensibly he is with Thomas Cook. He is a British agent. There is probably nothing much to worry about. It is maybe only a routine check-up on his part."

"Listen," I said. "That guy never found this place by tailing me here. He was nowhere in sight when I left the Maidan. How did he know I would come here and if so how much does he know about you and Gaby?"

There was a moment's silence. Pinel smashed out his cigarette in the ashtray on the desk.

"The Persian Cat," I said.

"Comment?"

"The customs guy, an Iranian, tried to make contact. I brushed him off."

Pinel made a gesture of impatience. "They would hardly be in league with Berkeley. Besides they would not have much interest in you. They exist only to achieve national unity and Iran's freedom from being a football in power politics. However, Berkeley undoubtedly has some native cohorts. You were probably trailed by one of his men."

"Listen," I said. "I wasn't being tailed, I've developed a sixth sense about that sort of thing. It's one of the perfected senses of the age in which we live."

Pinel looked enigmatic. He was being too damned careful not to register anything. Gaby was watching me in a puzzled manner. I knew what idea was occurring to both of them but I was worried about how seriously they took the idea. I decided to skip it for the moment.

We settled down to a discussion of plans for my entrance into Claire Fayne's life. At the end, Pinel said:

"You are not to return here until tomorrow night. And even that we may change. If we decide on another rendezvous I will get word to you. In the meantime..."

He stood and held out his hand, but there wasn't too much warmth in his handshake and he seemed preoccupied. I felt that he wished he had never suggested me to Caillaux.

Gaby walked with me through the rugs to the front door. The Iranian girl had not yet returned.

I remembered the present then, and dug into my breast pocket and opened the paper bag and held the nylons up and she squealed with delight.

"Tomorrow night," she said, "after Mrs. Fayne's party."

"Yes," I said.

"And not too late!" she said vehemently. I laughed pleasantly and went out into the empty hall. The plaster on the walls was cracked; a large spider scurried across the stained surface and disappeared into one of the cracks. When I emerged into the fading sunlight the man called Berkeley was nowhere to be seen.

I found a small French restaurant in the legation quarter and had an Italian meal with Arab overtones. Then I wandered around until I found a cinema and saw a picture, Al Jolson in "The Singing Fool." On one side of the screen

titles were flashed in French, on the other in Arabic. The
theatre was noisier than the sound track and had a faint reek
of stale urine. I left before the picture was half over and
walked slowly back to the hotel. The night was hot and filled
with the glare of naked electric lights and distant music and
harsh laughter. The hotel entrance was dimly lighted. The
lobby had the same abandoned appearance, containing only
an Arab porter and a pasty-faced young man who looked
up from behind the desk with syphilitic blankness.

When I asked the clerk for the number of Berkeley's room
he looked bored. But when I picked up the house phone
which was on the desk before him and although he turned
his back apparently busy with mail, I felt sure he was listening. The ringing of the phone had a lonely sound. When
there was no answer I hung up and went to the bar. Except
for the bartender, the place was empty. I ordered a cognac
and got something that tasted as though it had been aged in
the sewers of Paris. For an hour no one came into the bar.
Finally at ten o'clock I gave up and took the medieval elevator
up to the third floor. The moment I stepped out of the elevator, some gland took over; there was something here that
wasn't right. The elevator clanged down the shaft behind
me. The wide hall with its shuttered doors was lighted only
dimly. Up here all sound was muted and dreamlike. A
woman was screaming somewhere, far off, but of course it
might have been only an amorous cat.

As silently as possible I went to the door of my room, put
my head close to the shuttered panel and listened. There
was no sound. I waited about two minutes, taking the time
to examine the lock. It had not been tampered with. Then I
inserted the key, swung the door inwards and stepped quickly
to one side. Nothing happened. I curved my arm around
through the open door, found the light-switch and snapped
it down.

Yellow light trickled out into the corridor. I got out my automatic and stepped into the room. There was no sound of movement from either the room or the adjoining bath.

I closed the door behind me. My clothes were strewn about the floor, my bag lay open like a dead animal on the floor with ugly gashes through its lining. All the bureau drawers were wide open. A breath of hot air disturbed the curtains at the open window. Whoever had done the job was out in the open. There wasn't the slightest attempt to cover up. The air with heavy with the odor of sweet perfume.

And the Persian Cat stood in solitary aloofness on the bedside table.

I moved quickly to the phone but with one hand on the instrument changed my mind. I sat there on the small chair thinking it over.

I didn't hear anything, when it happened. I didn't feel a thing. There was just a sudden transition from light to darkness.

I opened my eyes to the glare of the bedside lamp. I closed them quick. There was a damp towel on my head. I smelled cigarette smoke. And the perfume was still there, very strong. I moved my hands to my pockets. They had been emptied. I opened one eye. Berkeley was sitting there beside the bed smoking.

"Good going, old chap," he said. "I thought for a time you weren't coming out of it. Who sapped you?"

I put my hand back to touch the lump behind my ear.

"Funny thing," I said, "the things some men get queer for."

"Like what?"

"Perfume."

He looked blank. "Never touch the stuff," he said.

"Some son of a bitch does. The room smelled like a whore house when I came in."

"Could have been a woman."

"Could. Maybe that's what I'm supposed to believe. Why did you do it, Berkeley? It wasn't necessary. I don't scare easy and I don't talk any better with a bump behind my ear."

"Wrong track, Denby. I didn't get back to the hotel until eleven. The clerk told me you had been trying to reach me and that you'd finally gone up to your room. When there was no answer on the house phone I decided to investigate."

All the time he was talking his eyes were on the Persian Cat.

"Nice bit of junk you've got there."

"Don't play dumb, Berkeley. You know as well as I do what it is. I only carry it for business reasons. My employer thought it might be helpful."

"It might also be dangerous," Berkeley said. "The right people might wonder how it got into the wrong hands."

"What did you want with me?"

He raised his eyebrows. It made him look as though he were in pain.

"If I'm not mistaken, old chap, you were the one who wanted to reach me. I was just curious."

"Yeah," I said. "That's why you've had a tail on me ever since I arrived."

"Yes," he said. "Just curious."

I indicated the bottle of scotch in the ruined bag. "Help yourself, And pour me one."

He obeyed languidly. Watching him I had a feeling of doubt. If he had been the one responsible for the condition of the room and the pain in my head he was just about the coolest number I'd ever come across. But there was something else about him, a pale cynicism, a feeling of death.

He handed me the glass with a strong shot in it and tipped the bottle up to his lips.

"Here's to the Oxford Group," he said. "Good idea those blokes have. Saves a lot of trouble, coming clean."

"You're in the wrong stall," I said. "I'm here to buy rugs for my employer in Chicago."

He laughed. "British Intelligence isn't that far gone," he said.

"Since when has British Intelligence set up an advertising bureau?"

He laughed some more. "I doubt if there's a European over twenty-one in this town who doesn't know about me. It's quite a trial now and then but I manage to get along."

"What I don't get," I said, "is if you didn't tap me behind the ear, who did and why? What had they to gain, my room had already been ransacked."

"Could be a Moslem idea of a practical joke," he said. Then he leaned forward and put the bottle on the floor beside him.

"Who are you working for, Denby? You'd better come clean, old chap. There are too many conflicting elements at work in this place as it is. Once this used to be a soft job. Not any more. Don't make it difficult for me."

"The Marshall-Stone Department Store in Chicago," I said. "Does that sound sinister?"

"Come, come. Let's drop the hop-scotch! I know more about you than you might expect. I suppose you were working for this Marshall-Stone when you did a job for the French in Syria? I suppose your O.S.S. training fitted you for the rug trade! Our London friends have you tabbed, Denby. You've been for sale ever since your discharge. What I want to know is, who's paying the checks now!"

"Marshall-Stone. If you don't believe it, you know what you can do. It's been nice having you. Thanks for the drink of my scotch and goodnight."

His small mouth became even smaller, tight and hard. "I'm not through yet," he said.

"I am." I threw aside the towel and got to my feet.

"Are you working for Edmund Marlan," he asked.

"Never met the boy. Although it's not a bad idea. I understand it's good work if you can get it."

He pushed back his chair and stood. He looked tired and suddenly bored. "All right, have it your way. Personally I think you're being a damned fool. If you came clean maybe I could help you. As it is," he shrugged, "whatever you are up to will be difficult to accomplish. I will see to it that you are immobilized."

"Am I being threatened by Britannia?"

"I didn't want it this way," he said.

He walked to the door and turned. He yawned. "Stay away from 14 Rue Beige."

"What's that?"

"Mrs. Fayne's house."

"Funny thing you should say that," I said coolly. "I understand there's a big party there tomorrow night. I'm a party boy from way back. Wouldn't miss it for the world."

I didn't wait to hear more but crossed the room, went into the bathroom and slammed the door. I took a shower and soaked my head in what passed for cold water. When I returned to the bedroom, Berkeley was gone.

And so was the Persian Cat.

Chapter 4

Though smaller than its neighbors, 14 Rue Beige was distinctly a woman's house, a gleaming jewel of a house set in a circle of lovely gardens. Two iron gates marked the entrance and exit of a semi-circular driveway and a long line of limousines was depositing guests at the entrance. A block away was the Boulevard des Ambassadeurs, the heart of the European colony.

I had walked from the Provençal. My only passport was that international uniform, a dinner jacket. Three heavy set

Iranian guards at the gate eyed me suspiciously but I walked through without being questioned. However, half way up the drive a huge man with a wrestler's curling moustaches and the face of a bull stepped out from the bushes and barred my way.

"You walk," he said, as though it were unheard of.

"Obviously."

He didn't budge. After a moment he leaned forward with a sadistic grin and jabbed a finger at my chest.

"You strong?"

I didn't bother to answer that one. He felt the muscles of my arm and before I knew it, lifted me off my feet as though I were a paper box and deposited me behind a bush, out of sight of the limousines on the driveway. I decided not to resist. A pal appeared from the darkness and quickly frisked me. I was thankful that I had decided to make this social call minus a rod.

"Satisfied?"

The wrestler, who wore the uniform of a chauffeur, grinned again and put out his hand as though he wished to show there were no hard feelings. His big paw closed on my hand like a vise. I smiled politely, brought down my heel sharply on his toes and when he slackened his grip in surprise, clamped his fingers together. He let out a high yelp.

"No hard feelings," I said, and let go. His pal muttered something in Arabic. He stood there trying to make up his mind whether to be angry or not. Finally he decided not to be and gave me the mechanical grin. "Go now," he said. I did, but quick.

I was lucky enough to reach the front door at the moment when a large party was stepping out of pre-war Mercedes and pushed through the entrance with them past the men at the door. In a moment I was standing in an archway to a large room that despite its many oriental touches might have been near the Etoile or in the Faubourg St.-Honoré. The place was crowded. Most of the men were in tails but there were enough black ties to keep me from being too conspicuous. From what I could gather, by a quick once-over, the English predominated. A roulette table in one corner was getting a good play. Ambassadorial foursomes were concentrating on bridge in alcoves. Paris gowns shimmered beneath the delicate crystal chandeliers and there was a generous display of diamonds and emeralds. A small orchestra of costumed Iranians played restaurant music in the gardens beyond the open window.

Automatically, a major-domo announced me. Several faces turned and looked in my direction but none of them were familiar to me. Mrs. Fayne didn't show so I hooked a glass of champagne and began to circulate, feeling like a private dick at a wedding where the gifts were expensive.

After a bit I became conscious that I was getting the eye from a couple of elegant looking boys. They were both very blond and for my money, very swishy. They stood behind, and seemed to belong to, an old man who sat in one of the alcoves holding court. The old man was plump but unhealthy looking, an old mogul ready for the grave but smiling a thin smile without humor or interest in it and all the time he smiled at the others he kept darting glances in my direction. Only his eyes seemed alive.

He turned and spoke to one of the fags. I turned away and pretended to be interested in the play at the roulette table. Someone tapped me on the shoulder. When I turned I wasn't surprised to find one of the blond boys.

"Pardon. I don't seem to know you."

"No," I said.

"You are here by invitation, of course."

"Of course."

"Really?" His eyebrows arched delicately.

"Really."

"Mrs. Fayne invited you?"

"Naturally."

For a moment he seemed stumped. I followed up quickly.
"Where is Mrs. Fayne?"

He thawed a little, still puzzled and obviously unsure.
"Your name, please?"

"Denby," I said glibly, "just tell her Gil Denby."

He moved back to the old man. Marlan, I thought. So
that's Marlan. He looked like a sick spider, in search of flies.

Through an open door I spotted a library. The book-lined
room was deserted. Easily, very casually, I walked into it. In
the center of the room was a large table loaded with Persian
Cats of all descriptions. One of the cats was a duplicate of
the one Berkeley had swiped from me. I went to the table
and picked it up.

Then I knew someone was watching me.

I waited a moment before I turned. A servant was standing
in the doorway with a tray of champagne glasses. Our eyes
met. I thought, let's see now. I put my thumb over the cat's
left eye and my index finger on the head spot. And, as he
moved forward to offer me a drink, I put the cat behind me
on the table. I took the champagne and waited. He moved
past me, picked up the cat and held his hand over it in the
same manner.

I gave him a blank look. "What's your name?"

"Ali Mohammed."

"Like Smith, eh? All right. Thanks, Ali." I drained the
glass and took another from the tray. "That's all for now."

He stood there, the smile fading from his lips and for just
a moment there was a flicker of something in his black eyes.
Uncertainty? Fear? Anger? I couldn't tell. I picked up the
cat and studied it again. I saw him stiffen and looked behind
me. I turned.

She was standing in the doorway wearing a gown of jade
green and around her neck was a fabulous diamond necklace.
She stood there, cool and chic, an expression of mild bewil-

derment on her face, more beautiful by far than her photograph had led me to expect. As I turned she took a small
backward step but the expression on her face didn't alter. I
figured that the resemblance to her dead husband hadn't
missed her. The servant faded away. She came towards me.

"Mr. Denby?"

I nodded. "I told them we had met to save trouble. Actually,
I'm a gate crasher."

"Oh?"

"I was a friend of Reggie's."

She stopped dead in her tracks. The social smile trembled
for a moment. She half turned as though to beat a retreat,
then changed her mind.

"But what an odd way to introduce yourself. You might
have called, you know."

"I didn't think you'd mind."

"Mind? But certainly I don't mind. I'm delighted to meet
a friend of Reggie's."

It was all automatic. I could see she was thinking fast. Or
trying to.

"Won't you sit down."

We sat. She on a tiny gilt chair, I on a delicate sofa. We
were about three feet apart.

"It's strange," she said. "But I don't recall Reggie ever
mentioning the name of Denby."

"It certainly is!" I said. "Considering that we were in the
same year at Christ College..."

"Oh, you knew him then!"

I could see the relief in her eyes.

"Of course he must have mentioned you. I'm frightfully
stupid about names."

"... and later," I said, "during the war. In Paris, after the
occupation."

She said nothing. The hand, holding a tiny mesh bag,
twitched. She looked from my face down at the Persian Cat

I still held. "Oh," she said bleakly, "I see."

"You're even lovelier than he said."

She didn't look up.

"Thank you." Then, after a moment. "In Paris..."

"And London. The Ministry of Information brought us together. You know, in many ways I wish Reggie had never gone into Secret Intelligence."

Her hands were working on the mesh bag.

"He was a brave man, though," I said. "His job saved a lot of lives."

She stood on that one. "Some other time we must talk about Reggie," she said. "Now you must meet some of my friends." Her voice was shaking.

"Please," I said. "I know it's selfish of me. But don't go back just yet."

"But I must..."

"I didn't mean to do this to you," I said. "A party is hardly the time for emotional reminiscences."

"Not at all." She was getting hold of herself. "But you know what these things are." She turned to me and looked directly into my eyes. "I must admit you gave me a turn when I first walked in. I suppose you know that your re-semblance to Reggie is extraordinary."

"So we were both told," I said. "I'd forgotten, though. I'm sorry."

"Please don't apologize. It was sweet and thoughtful of you to come. Now let me get you a drink and introduce you to some people..."

We started for the door. But halfway across the room she suddenly stopped and said, "Being a friend of Reggie's I suppose you feel you must in some way avenge his death?"

I took time to light a cigarette. "Come now," I said easily enough, "even Reggie would give a horse laugh to that one."

She gave me a startled look.

"After all," I went on, "we all want to forget that business.

What's done is done. There was enough ugliness to last a lifetime. Time to forget. I can hear Reggie saying, 'Don't be so solemn, old things, have fun.' "

"Fun?" Some of the tension went out of her face but she didn't smile. "But if you knew Reggie, you must have been doing some of the same sort of work?"

"No. I was in the American Army. O.S.S. But nothing spectacular, like Reggie. Right now I'm all for trying to forget the whole damned show. Actually, I came here to buy rugs for a Chicago department store."

She hesitated, then said, "I think you're right. It's better not to go on hating, isn't it?" Suddenly she smiled. Her eyes lit up. "After all, there is so much to live for. Reggie always adored fun."

But I thought the light in her eyes was too bright, even synthetically produced.

"I'm afraid, however, that Teheran is hardly a pleasure resort."

"I don't know," I said. "There are some things about it that fascinate me."

She stepped into her role like an old hand. "Perhaps you'll allow me to conduct you on a tour of the more fascinating spots one day."

I was about to say, "what day," when a voice behind us said, "Claire."

It was Marlan. In motion he had an air of elegance so exaggerated as to suggest a caricature of court manners.

"I must leave now, my dear," he said.

"I'm sorry, Edmund. I..."

"But I have not had the pleasure of meeting this gentleman."

Mrs. Fayne introduced us.

"I was a friend of Mrs. Fayne's late husband," I said.

"Indeed!" The hand which he had just withdrawn from mine felt like damp pulp. "I was very fond of Reggie, you know. A fine lad."

"Yes," I said casually.

"Then, of course, you're an old friend of Mrs. Fayne's..."

His English was impeccable but it might easily have been the English of a gifted foreigner who has mastered the language. His round-moon face betrayed no nationality. In fact it betrayed nothing.

"On the contrary," I began.

But Claire Fayne interrupted quickly.

"We never actually met, Edmund. He knew Reggie at Oxford. Friends wrote that Mr. Denby was coming to Teheran on business. Naturally, I sent the invitation to his hotel."

She was very smooth now, showing no nervousness. I wondered why she preferred Marlan to believe I had come at her invitation and why she had carefully omitted my knowing Reggie after the war had begun.

"So you're here on business, Mr. Denby?"

"Yes," I said, flatly, unequivocally, finally.

He smiled. "What business, if I may ask?"

"Rugs," I said.

"It is a pleasant surprise to meet one man at least who is here for other reasons than oil."

"It's a fill-in job," I said carefully. "I'll be looking for something better later on."

He took a jade cigarette holder from an inner pocket and ran his fingers over it but refused my offered cigarette. "There is plenty of opportunity here for the right man," he said. "Iran is no place for loafers or adventurers. But the chance is here for a man of intelligence, and..." his hesitation was slight, "initiative, shall we say?" Then suddenly he added, "Do I place a Texas accent?"

"Dallas," I said.

"Good Lord," Mrs. Fayne said. She looked at Edmund Marlan, a smile on her lips. Looked at him and yet through and beyond him. "I knew someone, a girl, who was born there. A long time ago," she mused.

"A fascinating country, the U.S.A.," Marlan said. "Full of extraordinary possibilities."

"Possibilities" seemed an odd way to describe my country. Marlan took my hand once more. Again I might have been holding a raw flounder.

"If I can be of service to you, Mr. Denby, do not hesitate to look me up. It would please me to be of assistance to any friend of... of... the Faynes."

I didn't miss the omission of Reggie's name. "The Faynes" sounded pretty much like a party of one consisting of only the fabulous Claire.

He slipped his arm through hers and good nights were said. Pressing his hand affectionately in hers, she led him out into the main room. I watched the two blond men close in almost military precision as they made their way to the foyer. Other guests bowed and called goodnight as Marlan passed but he disregarded them as though they were so many extras in a Hollywood production. Then I could see him in the hall, talking to Mrs. Fayne.

I looked around at the sleek, well bred company, not so sleek, not quite so well bred as it had been before the champagne began to flow. Now and then a raucous laugh, a too loud voice, a furtive hand on powdered skin struck a jarring note. And from the distance came the wild echo of the eastern city. It all seemed fantastically unreal on one plane, and yet utterly logical on another when one became adjusted to the fact that, in a nightmare, people behave like people in a nightmare.

And out in the hall, Claire Fayne went on talking with Marlan.

I thought, so far, so good. She was almost exactly what I had expected. Machine made. Off the same assembly line as Dorothy. Hard and chic and playing the game of sex with a dilettante's objectivity. It seemed incredible that this ornate palace, the Paris gowns and the servants were sufficient reward for going to bed with a monkey like Marlan. On the other hand, it seemed incredible, watching the mask faced old man, that there was any going to bed at all.

Someone took my elbow. "No sense of self preservation. Too bad." It was Berkeley, with nothing more formidable in his hand than a highball.

"Dull party," I said.

"I warned you it wouldn't be worth the effort."

"I'd be grateful to you," I said, "if you'd return that little souvenir you lifted from my room."

"Ah. The Persian Cat?"

"Yes."

"A matter of security, old chap. I don't want to see you dead before I fit you into the local puzzle."

"Haven't you been able to do that yet?"

"When I do, you'll have back your Persian Cat."

I signalled the waiter and obtained a fresh glass of champagne.

"What do you think of Marlan?" Berkeley said.

"What do you think?"

He shrugged. "A fantastic character. Ran a minor legacy into a fortune so large no one has been able to correctly estimate it. He was, and probably still is, a silent partner in many internationally known concerns. Before, and during the first years of the war, he was seen everywhere with a bodyguard that amounted to a private army. A house in London, and in Paris and in Mexico City and on the Riviera and even in Nassau. Hunting in Africa. Archaeology in China. The social season in New York. Boon companion of retired kings... and a couple of active ones. Now he seems to prefer Teheran. Have you seen his palace?"

"Not yet."

"An unbelievable page out of the Arabian Nights. Food and weekend guests flown in by private plane. Priceless antiques. Everything, in fact, but a harem."

"Apparently, paranoia sometimes pays off well," I said.

Berkeley sipped his drink, watching with jaundiced eyes the dialogue still taking place in the foyer.

"He wasn't too happy while you were having your tête à tête with Mrs. Fayne. Maybe it's because you look so much like her dead husband."

"How did you know that?" I asked quietly.

If he had had the blood, I believe he would have blushed. As it was, he gave a nervous little laugh.

"I once met Reginald Fayne. Saw the resemblance immediately I laid eyes on you. She was supposed to have been mad about him, you know. Marlan won't like ghosts at this point. Hot stuff. Mustn't touch."

I started to move away from him.

"Look, Denby," he said in a low voice, not letting me get away, "you'd better cooperate with me. I'm giving it to you straight. I have orders from the top and I intend to carry them out."

"There's nothing to cooperate about unless the British Government is in the rug business."

Marlan was leaving. Claire Fayne had turned back to the main room. I went quickly to her side.

"I've stayed long enough for a gate crasher," I said. "I'm going to take you up on that sightseeing offer. What day would be convenient?"

Her eyes were very cool. "I'm so sorry, Mr. Denby. I haven't a free moment all week. And next week I'm going up to the hills with friends. Perhaps if you are still here when I return..." She started to move past me.

But I blocked her way. "Listen," I said, "I'm not going to accept that. I couldn't survive that length of time."

"Don't be dull," she said sharply.

"Famous," I said, "you don't understand."

She stopped dead in her tracks, rigid with anger. "How

dare you call me that!"

"Oh come now, this isn't Victoria Regina. I've known you long before I ever met you. I dreamed about you last night. Do you want to hear..."

"What you need is an analyst, not a tourist guide. Good night."

I was aware of nearby faces turned to us in curiosity. I was standing close to her now. Very close. And I spoke in a low voice. "You're exactly what I need," I said.

She laughed. "Don't be an oaf!" And then she escaped, still laughing, to a group that parted to accept her. I waited a moment, watching her still. She manoeuvred around in the group until her face was visible once more. She still had that cold smile on her lips but she looked directly at me, eyes narrowed in a calculating, appraising manner. It was unmistakable.

I walked towards the entrance, feeling pretty good and at the same time filled with an almost destructive sense of fury.

A large black car was disappearing through the exit gate as I stepped out onto the dimly lit portico. A battered Daimler had just drawn up to the steps and a stout woman whose arms were covered with what might or might not have been diamonds was being helped into the rear by a young man with slick black hair. Down near the entrance gates I could see the three Iranian guards. A footman was in attendance, opening the doors of the limousine as they drew up. A group of three laughing women and a thin, high voiced man came out of the foyer. While the footman was busy with their car I stepped back behind one of the fat columns and made my way to the edge of the front terrace. In a moment I had dropped down amid the shrubbery.

The thin voice of the man came to me saying, "But you must admit, Celia, she does have chic!" Then a car door slammed and the car's motor purred louder as it swung out around the drive. Carefully I made my way along the side of the house behind the thick bushes. As I drew near the corner I could hear the music from the garden grow more distinct. I stood there a moment deciding on the next move. The music suddenly ceased. A woman's laugh rang out in the night. I crouched lower, afraid my figure would be discernible against the white facade. Above the lawns a pale moon, still as stone, hung in the hot sky.

Chapter 5

The last guest had departed an hour before. Now, gradually most of the lights on the first floor were being extinguished. The city had quieted down to the point where the sudden bray of a donkey sounded as clearly as a fire siren in the night. From my place of concealment behind a graceful little summer house in the depths of the garden I watched her silhouette cross and recross the silken curtains of the second floor bedroom. It would not be difficult to attain access to the room from which a French window opened on a balcony supported by delicate lacework columns.

Somewhere nearby there was the soft rustle of shrubbery. It might have been a night bird but I stayed where I was, as motionless as the china nymph in the center of the summerhouse. And then suddenly I heard something else, almost directly behind me. I wheeled about and struck out just in time. There wasn't even a struggle. I caught the dark face in midair and it fell in a heap of soiled brown cloth to the garden. Only the knife gleamed where it had fallen among the roses. Just to make sure, I bound and gagged the fellow in his own filthy clothes and left him where he had ruined the azaleas.

After that it was fairly easy sailing. The narrow, decorated columns offered an excellent means of reaching the balcony. The French windows were half open to catch whatever fugitive breeze might come down the night. Feeling rather absurd and wishing to hell I could remember the words of Bulldog Drummond under similar circumstances, I stepped down into the bedroom.

It was a place of satins and Louis Quinze and gilt candelabra and mirrors. But at the moment it was not a place of the Lady Claire. The sound of the shower through a half closed door told me where she was.

I made myself comfortable as possible on a silly little chair and lit a cigarette. Then I thought I would be at a disadvantage on the chair and moved to the chaise longue. When I was half finished with the cigarette she walked in. Not quite as I had expected, though. She was stark naked.

She stopped on the threshold. But if I lost some of my savoir faire, she lost none of hers. Quite calmly, and without undue haste she crossed to the bed, picked up a flimsy negligee and wrapped it about herself.

"And now," she said sweetly, "you will kindly get the hell out of here before I ring for the bouncer."

"I think I'll wait for the second show," I said.

"You certainly didn't pick up these crude tactics at Oxford."

"It's better than some of the things the other boys picked up."

She moved languidly towards the bell rope.

"Everyone likes to go to bed too early in Teheran," I said. "A party like the one just finished would be only getting under way in Paris. Couldn't we pretend this was the Rue Bl...?"

"The Rue Blanche?"

"Certainly not. I have a high opinion of you. Let's make it the Faubourg St. Germaine."

"You are either out of your mind or else you have a childish conception of the dramatic." But I noticed she veered away from the bell rope.

"A little of both and something else."

She went and sat on the bed. She put her hand to her fore-head in a sudden gesture of weariness and boredom.

"I'm too tired to play," she said. "Please go. I don't want a scene. I really can't cope with a scene."

I stubbed out my cigarette in the lap of a china nude. I leaned back and simulated a yawn.

"What do you want with me?"

"What did Marlan warn you I might want, when he was talking to you in the hall?"

"He believes you're some sort of an agent," she said candidly.

I hesitated. Then I said, "Well, in a way, he's right."

She looked up at me, her eyes suddenly tired and resentful.

"Will it never end!" she said.

Quickly I was reviewing the story Pinel and I agreed upon.

"Harry Altmont is in trouble," I said.

"Altmont?" She looked puzzled.

"Vichy," I said. A light of sudden recognition came into her eyes. She stood and moved nervously towards a cigarette box on the bedside table. She had her back to me.

"He's being held in Algiers. There's some doubt about his loyalty during those years at Vichy. He was a friend of Reggie's, you know. I thought you might be able to clear him of, what most of us believe to be, a trumped up charge. You certainly are in a position to vouch for his loyalty, even his heroism."

She didn't turn. "I remember him. It seems long ago." Her voice was entirely mechanical.

"And he was a good man."

She dropped the cigarette back into the box. When she turned her face was hard and set.

"Good?" she asked. "Who am I to say! The hell with all that. It's past. Finished. I want to forget it."

I was thinking, why am I getting angry. That's me talking.

Me talking from her lips. Me sitting across the table from Pinel. But all the same I felt a wave of fury.

"They might shoot him," I said. "They might put him up before a firing squad and pour bullets into him. Doesn't that matter to you?"

"Maybe he is a traitor," she said in a hard voice. "A lot of the 'good ones' turned out not so good. I don't know the 'good ones' from the bad ones any more and frankly I don't give a damn!"

"You're so pretty for such a bitch," I said.

"This is fantastic! Get out! Leave me alone!"

I waited a moment, then said, "They'll execute him. You could save him."

"No!" But her hands were clenched tightly together.

"The charge against him is that during a certain period he was working for the Nazis. In Dijon, 1944. And we understand he was actually living under the name of Paul Rouget in Vichy."

"What difference does it make where he was! He could have been working with the Germans from Vichy. He would have been with the majority."

"This is a specific charge. Was he or was he not in Vichy?"

She started to pace back and forth. Finally she returned to the cigarette box and this time lit up with a shaking hand. When she sat down again on the edge of the bed I saw that she was attempting to get hold of herself.

"I'm very tired," she finally said carefully. "This sort of party with a lot of stupid people milling about exhausts me. I used to like it. When it was new." She caught herself up. "I didn't quite mean all I said. Naturally if I can do anything to help Harry Altmont I would be delighted to help."

"You would be willing to give us a statement?"

She hesitated a moment. Then, looking me in the eye, she bowed her head.

I swung my legs over the edge of the chaise longue and

leaned forward. I hadn't expected such ready acquiescence. I decided to take advantage of her mood and work fast.

"It means going to Algiers for the trial," I said.

Her head jerked up and she looked at me sharply. "That's absurd," she said. "And you know it! I'll give you a deposition before a notary or whatever they call it, but I can't go to Algiers. It's quite impossible."

"Altmont's friends are willing to meet your expenses. It would mean only three days away. You could get an Air France plane on..."

"It's not the money!"

"What then?"

Impatiently she blew a thin stream of smoke out into the room.

"I simply don't want to be mixed up in it. If a sworn statement isn't satisfactory, I can't do any more."

"Surely," I said deliberately, "you're not afraid to go?"

She was in command again. "Why should I be afraid?"

I waited. She outlasted me, even managing a derisive little smile.

"Funny," I said carefully. "Listening to Reggie talk, I saw you as a different sort of person."

She didn't bat an eyelash. "Did you? I was a little more naïve in those days, Mr. Denby. Really, you shouldn't try so hard to put me in a bad light."

"I'm not trying to," I said. I looked up at her slowly. "Now I'll be the one who is naïve. It may sound corny to you but you've been on my mind for a helluva long time. And after meeting you tonight. You know Reggie told me so much. The month at St. Moritz. The climb on the Matterhorn."

The smile faded from her lips and the color was leaving her face. "That was another life," she said tonelessly. "Finished. Done."

I didn't let up. I dragged up all the business I had got from Pinel. All the little details that obviously were cutting into her as though I wielded a knife. At the end I said, "but I'm not Reggie."

She looked away. "No, you're not Reggie. You're trying to save Harry Altmont."

There was something strange in the way she said it, something bitter and lost.

"What are you trying to say?"

She stood now and I saw fright in her eyes. "You must go now. Ell—I'll think it over. About Algiers, I mean."

"Were you about to imply that Reggie..."

"Nothing. I must talk to Edmund. You see..."

"You mean to tell me you intend to discuss our conversation with Marlan?"

"Why not?" She looked at me searchingly.

I shrugged meaningfully.

"Edmund is the only friend I have in the world," she said. "The only man I really trust. You only know him through the yellow press. He's not like that. You don't know some of the things he did during the war. He knows everything. Everything."

She was trying to convince me. Or was it herself. I played on the doubt far back in her eyes. Silently. With my eyes.

"Of course I'm going to tell Edmund!" she burst out angrily. "And furthermore..."

I stood up and began to walk towards her. I was thinking, hell, it's part of the job. Forget the other. You can't be a heel in this business. I walked towards her and she backed away. She didn't try to dart past me or call out. She merely kept backing up until the wall was behind her and could go no further. She didn't try to fight me but it was worse than that. There was a sort of utter despair in the way she allowed my arms to encircle her. I was thinking in one part of my mind, you filthy murdering bitch, you Dorothy, you... And in the other part, I was thinking, Good Christ, it's never been like this before.

Her eyes were closed, and she whispered, "Reggie..."

I drew her close to me. The negligee was slipping from her shoulder.

There was a knock on the door.

Chapter 6

I moved faster than the romantic lead in a French bedroom farce, out through the French windows to the small balcony where, flattened against the white stone wall I got a good view of the room. Claire Fayne got on the bed with a book in her hand before she called out, "Come in." I couldn't understand why it should annoy me that she played the scene as though she had plenty of previous performances to her credit.

Marlan came in. Right away the mood of the tableau changed. In appearance he was not unlike the aging cuckold of the French farce, but there was something in his manner that suggested grand guignol undertones. Smooth as old amber, aging Europe, ferocious in his weariness, claws concealed beneath velvet. His voice, when he spoke, made me think of parchment.

"Forgive me, my dear. I saw your light. There are some things I wished to discuss with you."

"How odd, Edmund. You might have telephoned, you know." But her voice was just a bit too high pitched. The surprise too artificial. I watched him closely. If he got the warning in her voice, he betrayed no sign of it.

"May I sit for a moment?"

"Please do."

I had him in profile now. His head moved imperceptibly. I felt, rather than saw, him taking in the room. After a moment my gaze was drawn to the ashtray. I looked up quickly to see Claire staring without expression at the book by her side. Marlan took his time.

"Who has been smoking here," he finally asked. Very mild. Only a faint and rather bored interest.

"Smoking," she laughed. "I know you don't like me to smoke. But tonight, well, tonight." She shrugged, as though the thought were hardly worth finishing.

"Tonight you were nervous," he said.

"A little. I loathe these large brawls. Hang a lamb chop to the chandelier and all the world to dinner, you know."

Marlan picked up one of the cigarette stubs and stared at it thoughtfully. "Some time you must tell me how you manage to smoke one cigarette on which there is the trace of lipstick and keep the others free of it."

She didn't bat an eyelash. "I smoked the first one before I bathed. After that I used the cigarette holder Reggie gave me." Quite calmly she picked up a jade holder from the bedside table and laughed again. "Edmund! My dear. Of course I didn't use a holder. Those are the traces of my departed lover. The Captain of the Guards!"

Obviously not amused, he shrugged in his turn. "I don't think I should mind 'the Captain of the Guards.' That sort of thing has its place. As long as I know about it, of course."

There was a silence. A chill started down my spine. She was lying back against the headboard, a small smile on her lips, indifferent as far as I could see to the meaning of his words. The silks and gilt and mirror glistened in the soft light.

"I came to talk to you about the young American," he finally said.

"American? Oh, you mean Mr. Denby?"

"Denby, yes." He sighed. "He is not merely a 'Captain of the Guards,' my dear. I would find no pleasure in your receiving him."

She stifled a yawn. "Surely, Edmund, darling, you didn't come here merely to tell me that. Not at this hour!"

"He is very much like Reggie!" There was a sudden edge in his voice.

"I noticed the resemblance."

"Perhaps that is warning enough."

She looked worried. As far as I could see she was not giving him any warning in pantomime, but I couldn't be sure. She got up and began to pace back and forth. "Do you remember Harry Altmont, Edmund?"

Marlan sat still as a statue for a moment, then ran his chubby hand across his forehead in a weary fashion.

"So. That is what this Denby talked to you about."

"In the library," she said quickly. "He told me that Altmont was in some sort of trouble."

"And he wanted your help?"

"Well..."

Marlan got slowly to his feet. He came towards the window. I backed up against the wall. He stood there two feet from me, staring out into the night. He talked over his shoulder. "You are to stay out of this, Claire. You know what happened once. A man like Altmont, he might be anything."

Claire said nothing. Marlan's breathing, so near me, had a rasping sound.

"You agreed to trust my judgment in these things, Claire."

"Yes." Her voice sounded far away.

Suddenly I was convinced that all this had been for my benefit. Marlan knew I was on the balcony, Claire had given him some sort of a signal. They wanted me to believe in Claire's naïve doubt about Altmont.

And suddenly a tired whisper reached my ears. It seemed to float out of the flimsy curtains in the window.

"Stay out of it if you wish to live."

For a moment I thought it must have been my imagination. A hot breeze was springing up in the night. Below me the foliage rustled. Marlan was still there in the window, his shadow fell across the balustrade. It seemed incredible that it had been Marlan speaking. I thought of Claire Fayne near the peach colored silk of the bed and the aging vulture between us. I thought of Gaby and the man called Altmont, and Reggie Fayne lying dead on the floor of a drawing room in Vichy, and the woman smiling across the powdered shoulders and glittering jewelry in the room below. And I thought of her as she had walked naked across the bedroom, unconcerned, bored even, sick with her own corruption. Or, made sick by the corruption of the world about her.

The shadow on the balustrade flowed down the railings, retreated back across the balcony floor, trickled out of sight. I stayed there, hearing him say good night, stayed there flat against the wall until I heard the click of the door.

She was standing in the center of the room, her hands clasped together, waiting for me. I stopped on the threshold of the French windows.

"Your first name?" she asked.

"Gil."

"Come back, Gil."

"I'll be back," I said. And I said to myself, I'll be back all right, you bitch, you murdering, two-timing, cold blooded bitch.

"You heard. He thinks Altmont..." She stopped. She was frowning.

"Well?"

"He thinks... Oh, Gil, I'm so mixed up. It's been like that for a long time. I need to talk to you. For a long time."

"Tomorrow?"

"Call me in the morning. We must be careful. I understand Edmund. I'm sorry for him. But he's dangerous. We must be careful."

"Don't worry." I started across the room to her. She backed away.

"Don't touch me now," she said. "Tomorrow."

I turned but before I could reach the windows she had

rushed to my side and clutched my arm.

"Gil. Reggie. You were with Reggie before he died?"

"Yes."

"I don't want to believe that. I must believe you didn't know."

"I don't know what you mean."

The bleakness of my voice struck home. She let go of my arm and backed away. She went to the bed and sat there and when she spoke her voice was tired and bored. "Please go now."

I left her sitting there like a jewel in an expensive box and stepped over the threshold once more. Teheran lay crouching in the moonlight.

Chapter 7

A bell was tolling. A harsh, metallic sound like an iron hammer on an anvil. The black crooked street behind the Maidan-i-Mashq was deserted. I moved through it as I moved through all my life these days—alone, on guard, aware of the violence in all the nightmare about me. I thought of the woman I had left behind in the luxurious European house. Hard and brutal, a product of her times, living for the main chance even though it meant murder to attain her end. I wondered if the time would come when Dorothy might find murder standing between her and her selfish needs, and if so, whether or not she would take the same choice that Claire had taken. And I thought also, with a kind of fury, who the hell am I to moralize. This is a job. No more. A job in a world of filthy jobs.

The narrow street curved sharply and there around the bend the darkness was disturbed by a garish electric sign consisting of naked electric light bulbs spelling out CHEZ LAUTREC.

Blank walls rose on either side, pierced here and there by a heavy door. From the entrance to the Chez Lautrec came the faint sound of music, dream music, dissonant and, despite its barbaric beat, poignant as a lost moment. I went beneath an arch, opened a blue door, descended a narrow stairway and found myself in a small room, choked with smoke, reeking of garlic and coffee and sweat, reverberating with the wail of violins and throbbing drums. There were dim lanterns and candles on the tables. A few motheaten Europeans, who had the appearance of discouraged clerks, sat nursing their drinks while the good Moslems sipped at coffee and stared stolidly at a dark, animated and bare girl who held the center of the small floor.

A beady-eyed Frenchman with a thin three inch cigar dangling from one corner of his mouth was doing his accounts at a platformed desk marked "CAISE." He was in shirt sleeves and needed a shave.

"Speak English?" I asked.

He squinted at me and then, after an insolent moment, nodded.

"I'd like to see Lautrec."

He exposed an inch of rotting teeth.

"Behold him, Monsieur." He pointed the quill pen at himself.

"Where can I find Pinel?"

He shrugged. "Sit down. Wait here. Who knows?"

He slid out from behind the desk and shuffled towards the back of the room. I found a table in the native section between two men from the desert who were obviously startled at the dancer's nakedness, but were accepting it just the same as a normal aspect of the metropolis. The dancer was doing classic things with her stomach. Her arms were covered with brass bracelets that jingled as she moved about. She gave me her best smile. Her best was none too good.

The jaundiced looking Europeans in their crumpled whites

sat about behind fly-specked tables looking for all the world like the remnants of a defeated race. Lautrec returned bringing with him a drink. He bent down and said, "Pinel is waiting for you."

"Where?"

"Follow the girl when the dance ends. It will be helpful if you also let her see you smile upon her."

He left me and I gave the girl a Pepsodent advertisement. Her face lighted up hopefully. But the dance went on and on. The drum kept up the same relentless rhythm. The room seemed devoid of air. The silence of the men at the tables was unnatural.

I took a sip of the ghastly drink and then, as I placed the glass back on the table, looked up to see Berkeley coming in from across the street.

He spotted me immediately and snaked his way across the room between the tables. "Doing the town, old boy?"

"Don't sit down," I said. "I was just leaving."

He dropped into the next chair and gave me an urbane smile.

"This is as good a place as any for a quiet chat," he said. "No understanding ears on either side of us."

"Why the hell can't you guys work an eight hour day?"

"Am I wrong in concluding that you are working for Marlan?"

"Dead wrong. I saw him for the first time tonight." Over Berkeley's shoulder I saw Lautrec, head cocked to one side behind his desk, beady eyes, blank face frozen in Berkeley's direction.

"Then you're with the Russians." He was emphatic.

"Dja," I said.

"It might possibly be too late for you, Denby, by the time you get around to giving the right number."

"I like games. As a matter of fact, if we had a deck of cards..."

"The game you're playing is for keeps, Denby." He wasn't smiling now.

"Too late at night to go around threatening people, Berkeley."

"I'm the least of your dangers here. You must be dumber than I thought."

"Not dumb. Just indifferent."

He leaned towards me. "Look, lend lease. If this is a come-on game for Marlan, watch the way you deal. He's allergic to the strip tease method. Get everything off quickly and come to the point if you want to stay in a breathing condition."

"That's colorful talk for an old school tie. However, if I decide to fish in Marlan's part of the lake, I'll take your advice."

The music ended abruptly. I looked at my watch. It was two-thirty. The dancing girl had turned off her artistry as if by a switch and was walking flatfootedly through the tables to the rear of the orchestra platform.

I got up. "Excuse me. I have a date."

Berkeley shrugged. "Tourist stuff, but I'll wait."

The girl hesitated at the door, looked back over her shoulder, smiled invitingly and disappeared, leaving the door ajar behind her. I stepped over the threshold into a combination dressing room and bedroom. It was a dismal, evil smelling room. Pinel was sprawled on the bed reading a newspaper. Another dancing girl was completing her makeup at the dressing table. My decoy had turned to me questioningly, standing there in the center of the room like a mechanical device.

Pinel put down the paper.

"Meet Nara," he said. "The other one is Shara. They live here. You couldn't find better girls. They speak neither English nor French."

Shara, the girl at the mirror, went out to the fresh music.

Nara glowered at me hopefully while I sat on the bed beside Pinel. After a moment she shrugged and plopped herself down on the floor where she continued to watch us like a sleepy kitten.

I offered Pinel a cigarette. He refused. He didn't say anything and then after a moment he took a sodden pack of cigarettes from his own pocket and carefully lighted up. I didn't like it.

"You are late," he finally said.

"Strictly business. La Fayne."

"Ah yes. I sincerely hope it was the business for which you originally contracted. For your sake, as well as ours."

"All right, baby," I said in sudden anger. "There's no use playing along this way. If you don't trust me."

"I trust you but I worry."

"As far as I'm concerned you..."

"Waste of time!" His voice was sharp. "What happened?"

I gave him a full report of the evening. He seemed puzzled when I told him of Claire Fayne's agreeing to help Altmont.

"It's a trick," he said.

"That's what I thought. She's been playing innocent. The whole scene with Marlan in her bedroom was played for my benefit. He knew I was out there all the time."

Pinel looked down at his cigarette. I could see he was disturbed and at the same time uncertain. After a moment he gave it to me. "Why did you make an appointment to meet Berkeley here?"

"I didn't make an appointment. I have no idea how he discovered I was to be here."

"How much did he offer you?"

"For what?"

Pinel shrugged cynically. "That is what I would like to know."

"I'm beginning to feel as though I had a persecution complex," I said. "I'm working for you, Pinel. I'm not listening to anyone's offers. As a matter of fact, Berkeley hasn't made me an offer. He's just curious and full of dire warnings."

"Ah?"

For the first time, Pinel looked directly into my eyes. The veil was gone and I saw something there very much like pain.

"You know, Denby. While I waited for you I was remembering the night we blew up the troop train. Do you remember what we discussed that night while we were in the ditch?"

"No," I said harshly. "Anyway, whatever it was, it was then. Lots of things have changed since then."

"Gil," he said softly, "give yourself a chance before it is too late."

"How about sticking to business?"

He gave up then and smashed out his cigarette on the floor beside the bed and swung his legs over the edge and looked away from me.

"When do you next see Mrs. Fayne?"

"Tomorrow."

"You must work fast. If Marlan is suspicious of you, which seems to be the case, you must persuade her to go to Algiers as soon as possible. Perhaps it can be worked out as a romantic trip. N'est-ce pas? A private plane. Three nights alone together. That's your problem."

"I'll do my best."

"And stay away from Gaby."

"Maybe I'm hard of hearing." I was on my feet when I said it. "I didn't get that last." I turned to him.

"That's an order," he shouted. Nara looked up at us with a worried expression.

I told him where he could put that order, and started for the door.

"Watch out, Denby! That's a warning!"

"Everybody is full of warnings tonight."

I went out into the main room slamming the door behind

me. Berkeley was gone. Shara was rolling her stomach around for the late customers. The drums were still on the same monotonous rhythm. The faces of the Europeans looked like faded wrapping paper in the yellow light. The eyes of the Moslems were blank.

Chapter 8

The vast square of the Maidan Tupkhaneh was almost completely deserted. On the far side an occasional shadow slid along the walls but all about me were shuttered coffee shops and upturned coffee tables. The dome of the mosque was luminous in the moonlight and some sort of a night bird hovered over the square, flapping its enormous wings lethargically. Suddenly it uttered a harsh, almost human cry and went gliding off to the east.

Ever since I had left the Chez Lautrec a certain anxiety had been with me. Berkeley's disappearance, Pinel's suspicious attitude, the inexplicable sensation of a net closing about me. I wondered whether Gaby would reflect any of Pinel's suspicions. Better explain.

And then I thought, explain what? After all was not Pinel essentially right? The confusion that had been with me increased. I thought maybe a talk with Gaby can straighten things out.

I moved around the square, keeping close to the walls. Once I ducked into a doorway and looked back. There was no one there. Even the shadows had disappeared. Finally I turned off the square into the Rue Revjed and in a few minutes stood before the building I had visited earlier in the day. The façade was dark as a tomb but I remembered that the offices of Siraud et Cie were in the rear. Gaby had said that she would wait for me.

A car turned into the Rue Revjed from the square and I

quickly ducked into the entrance. The car crept slowly down along the curb but just as it got opposite me it picked up speed and went roaring off. It was a Rolls town car and although the rear seemed empty I could just make out two dim figures in the front. I lit a match and found the Siraud card with the bell beneath it. I rang and put my hand on the knob of the main door. To my surprise the door was already open. I didn't wait for the buzzer but went right in and hurried up the wooden stairs. There was one dim light burning on the second floor hall. At the end the glass panel of Siraud et Cie glowed faintly. For a moment I stood there listening. There was utterly no sound in the building. Revolver in hand, I opened the door and entered the office with its roll-top desk and many rugs. "Gaby!"

Silence. My heart was beating violently now. A lamp was burning in the back office. Cautiously I moved between the rugs. The palms of my hands were damp, this room of hanging rugs seemed full of ominous shadows. The part of my mind that was working kept saying, she's gone. Of course she forgot to turn off the light in the back office when she left. There's no one in there.

I pushed open the door and stepped into the little rear room. A weak bulb burned in the lamp on the desk. Gaby was on the floor, huddled up against the divan, her head fallen crazily to one side, eyes wide and fixed. Her hand was stretched towards me as though in supplication.

A shutter began clicking on and off in my mind. This is real, this is not real, this is real, this is not real. And then the clicking began to slow down, despite an agonizing effort of the consciousness to sustain it, and it began to go. This is, this is not, this is, this is not, and finally: this is real.

Gaby broken and dead. Gone. Destroyed.

My glands began to play tricks on me, spilling a toxic condition into my blood stream, flooding me with almost overpowering weariness. Standing there in the doorway with the

French girl at my feet, the memory of her courage and gaiety bright upon me, I felt a despair more intense than any I had ever known.

Only dimly was I aware of the overturned filing case and the papers littered about the desk. Or the broken china cat on the floor beside Gaby. Or the faint, very faint odour of perfume hanging on the air.

Somewhere behind me in the building there was a small sound. A door closing? The furtive movement of an animal? It didn't seem important. Gaby was gone. This was a rag doll on the floor.

I must have stood there a long time before the anger began. It was almost a physical sensation, creeping up from my toes, shuddering across my stomach muscles, filling my throat and head, leaving me trembling. Anger is too mild a word. It was a fury such as I had never known, even during the worst days of the war.

I resisted the impulse to lift Gaby and place her on the couch, thinking of finger prints, and turned my back on the room. I went out into the gloom of the main room and stood there among the rugs for a moment, trying to get hold of myself. In the last few minutes my little rational world had collapsed around me. My bargain basement cynicism, my detachment, my determination to do a job without feeling. I had a job all right. But it wasn't the check that mattered any more. It was simply to get my hands around the throat of the person who had broken Gaby's neck.

Chapter 9

Now even the shadows had gone from the city's streets and squares. The populations might have been destroyed by some atomic scourge and the moon was sinking in the west. By the time I reached the entrance to the Provençal I had thrust my anger far down within me so that my mind might be free for action.

The entrance door was locked. I found the night bell and pressed it. As I waited there I was aware again of some distant sound, furtive and barely audible, the sort of a sound I had heard as I stood on the threshold of the back office staring down at Gaby's body. I pivoted quickly about. No one was in sight but the hairs on the back of my neck warned me and I jumped to one side. There was a sharp crack, like a whip being snapped, a hissing sound near my ear and then the soft ping as the bullet buried itself in the heavy wood of the door frame.

Chains rattled. The door swung back and I slipped quickly inside the lobby past the surprised night porter. He gave me a puzzled look as he replaced the chains. I went right to the desk, picked up the house phone and called Berkeley's room. The night clerk stared at me impassively. When there was no answer I hung up and asked, "Hasn't Mr. Berkeley come in yet?"

"Berkeley?" He stifled a yawn. "You must mean the Englishman, Monsieur."

"Yes."

"M. Berkeley, he check out early this evening."

"Checked out! Where was he going?"

"He catch the eleven o'clock plane for Aberdajan."

Either the clerk was lying or Berkeley had deceived him, to say the least. I had seen the Englishman in Lautrec's place long after midnight. As I stood there trying to figure where Berkeley fitted into Gaby's murder, the clerk turned to the pigeon holes behind him and took out an envelope.

"A message for you, Monsieur."

I took the note from him and tore it open. It read,

"Please phone me when you receive this note. The lateness of the hour will not matter. E. Marlan." Automatically, I reached for the phone on the desk then changed my mind, bade the clerk goodnight, signalled to the porter and went to the elevator. Arrived in my room I grabbed the phone directory and in a few moments, after a servant had taken my name, was talking with Marlan.

"I am delighted that you called," he said pleasantly.

"I took you at your word about the lateness of the hour."

"Excellent. I trust for my own pleasure that you too suffer from insomnia, Mr. Denby. The night is much the most pleasant time. Perhaps you would do me the honor of joining me in a night cap. The view of the sunrise is really extraordinary from my place."

"That sounds pleasant," I said, as though it were the most natural thing in the world to accept an invitation for a drink at four a.m.

"Splendid!" There was genuine pleasure in his voice. He wanted me out there bad. But it couldn't have been as bad as my desire to go. "I'll send a car for you immediately," he said.

After I hung up I sat there trying to clear the cobwebs from my brain. It was all a bit too glib, the note being there, the telephone call, the invitation. A bit too easy. I wondered if it had been Marlan's men who had shot at me in the street.

I looked up Lautrec's number and picked up the phone. The instrument rang for a long while on the other end and I was just about to give up when Lautrec' voice came on. "Well?"

"American Embassy? Mr. Wilson, please," I said.

Lautrec was silent, aware of course, that all this was for the benefit of whoever might be listening in.

"Well," I continued, "just give Mr. Wilson a message for me, will you. Keep that poker game going, tell him I've got to stop and see Edmund Marlan, and..."

Lautrec interrupted harshly, "That is no surprise to us!"

"Listen," I said. "Hold on, you don't get it."

But the phone went dead. I slammed down the instrument

in a sudden rage. The god damned fools suspected me of selling out to Marlan. They... And then I caught my breath. Did they know already about Gaby? Did they, could they think that I...

With shaking fingers I extracted a cigarette and lit up. Surely not. Pinel knew the way things had been between Gaby and me. Even if he had been suspicious of me, afraid I might sell out to a higher bidder, he certainly couldn't think I had anything to do with Gaby's death.

And yet...

I was no longer so positive that Marlan had instigated that abortive assassination in front of the hotel. I found the light switch, plunged the room into darkness and went to the windows. Down at the end of the street, shadows were lurching across the lighted space between the buildings like figures on a dimly lighted stage, a camel caravan creeping into the city. I stood there puffing at the cigarette, knowing that I was waiting for the sound of the phone and Pinel's voice, and yet also knowing it would never come.

The phone rang sharply. I snatched it up. But it was only the night clerk.

"Mr. Marlan's car is waiting for you, M. Denby." His voice was far more servile than I had heard it before.

"I'll be right down." When I stepped out of the elevator the blond fag who had approached me in Mrs. Fayne's house rose from one of the wicker chairs and came towards me smiling.

"Mr. Marlan asked me to escort you. Incidentally, I'm Nils Drexel."

I nodded shortly, discouraging his outstretched hand and followed him out to the front of the hotel. A black Rolls town car was waiting at the curb. It looked very much like the one I had seen in the street before going up to the offices of Siraud et Cie. The man at the wheel was the burly wrestler in chauffeur's uniform who had accosted me as I walked up the driveway to Mrs. Fayne's house. He turned slightly, gave me a blank stare and then resumed his frozen, eyes front attitude. I stepped into the rear of the car with Drexel behind me. Almost immediately I caught the faint reek of perfume.

Drexel sat beside me and lighted a cigarette. The car drew away from the curb. I was pretty sure Drexel wasn't the source of the perfume.

"What scent does the chauffeur use?" I asked. "It's very pleasant." I minced just enough.

Drexel looked puzzled. "Scent?" He said he didn't understand. He sniffed. Then he smiled. "That isn't Haussan, I assure you."

"Who uses it?"

He lifted his eyebrows. His voice was arch. "Perhaps I shall tell you someday. Strange we never ran into one another in Paris, old man. You *must* have been there before the war."

I played along with him. The trip seemed longer than it probably was. But I couldn't find out who it was that used the perfume. However I was fairly certain now that the person who had conked me on the head and later murdered Gaby was one of Marlan's boys.

The car swerved off the main road. Ahead of us a white palace glistened on a moonlit hillside. I was aware of gates closing behind us and the feeling of having stepped into something out of the Arabian Nights. Even at this hour uniformed guards stood at attention before the terrace and footmen in costumes that were once familiar to Haji Baba appeared at the arched portals of the main entrance.

"What's this, the swing shift?" I couldn't resist asking Drexel. I got a pained look for my trouble and began to feel better. He led the way down a tiled foyer lined on one side by delicate columns which supported arches opening into a garden where fountains splashed in the moonlight, into a reception room whose desks, telephones and lights reminded me that I was after all not in another century.

He asked me to take a chair, indicated cigarettes and a decanter of liquor and glasses. I was already helping myself to a stiff drink as he disappeared through large double doors that were opened from the other side for him by two bodyguards without an apparent signal. Marlan seemed to go in for more personal protection than the King of England.

I sat down with my drink and began to plan my strategy. I was fairly certain that Marlan, suspecting I was doing a job he didn't want done, was going to attempt to buy me off. It would probably be done in a smooth, gentle manner—an offer of work with him—but I knew damn well the claws would be there all the time. I had to take the chance that he didn't know I already knew about Gaby. Otherwise he might not be too convinced of my willingness to play ball with him.

I wasn't working for Pinel now. This was on my own from now on out. And I intended to get that bitch, Claire Fayne!

The foyer door opened and a young man strolled in. He was the other pretty boy who had been standing next to Marlan at Claire Fayne's party. He stopped inside the door.

"Oh, I'm so sorry," he said delicately. "I didn't know..."

"That's all right."

The scent was there. It had come into the room with him. Carefully I put my glass down on the table beside me. I even managed a smile.

"That's nice perfume," I said. "What is it?"

He froze. For a moment he stared at me in consternation, then his eyes darted to the panel of the door through which Drexel had disappeared.

"I... I don't know what you're talking about."

"Oh come now," I heard myself saying in dulcet tones, "don't be so modest. As a matter of fact I'm a great fancier of good perfume."

He looked uncertain for a moment and then smiled boyishly. I managed to stay put in my chair, to keep my fists still and the encouraging smile on my face.

He came closer to me with a conspiratorial look on his face. "Promise you won't breathe a word about it."

"Oh, no."

"I'm very much afraid I lifted it," he said archly.

"Oh? From whom?"

"From Mr. Marlan. He'd be furious if he knew! You mustn't tell."

"Scout's honor."

"Well, you see, I have a *thing* about perfume. I suppose Krafft-Ebing or Freud or one of those dreadful characters have some explanation of it but I *do* think it's dull to know *why*, don't you?"

"Definitely."

"Well, a case of it came in from Cairo last week. I couldn't resist taking a bottle. He wouldn't mind, you know, it's only, I do think it's desperately funny, don't you?"

"It's a scream. I didn't know he used it."

"Mr. Marlan! Oh dear, it's not his, I mean not for his own personal use. He has it made up in Cairo for Mrs. Fayne."

Somehow I managed to keep the grin on my face. I even found my hand moving mechanically to the glass of whisky. I kept my eyes on him. If he was lying he was doing a beautiful job. But I couldn't be sure. Everything about him was so unreal that it would be difficult to tell when he was being honest. Close up, his face, so like a corrupt choir boy, had the texture of dough. His hands fluttered about like lost birds.

It was simply inconceivable that Claire Fayne had hit me on the head in my room or murdered Gaby. It wasn't the way a woman like that worked. And yet it was equally farfetched to imagine that this fluttering case of arrested development could have sustained such grim work. For the first time I wondered whether the perfume was not a blind.

He was talking. Too near. I wished to hell he'd go away.

"Now then. It's such a delightful way to begin a friendship.

With a secret. It's like a pact, almost. I'm Roddy Grayle.
When I saw you tonight at Mrs. Fayne's I just knew they
couldn't be right about you."

"They?"

"Oh, Nils Drexel." His face became petulant. "I really
can't bear him any more. Nils was trying to make Mr. Marlan
believe fantastic things about you."

"I can believe it of Nils," I said with sympathy in my voice.
"What did he say?"

"Oh, some utterly utter things about your working for the
British or the French or the Russians. I really can't remember
which. Honestly I began to think of you as a James Mason
sort of person, you know."

"You flatter me. Are you British, Roddy?"

"Everyone thinks I am. I wish I were, really. So much more
tone, you know. Actually I had the misfortune to be born in
Iowa. My father was a plumber there. A horrid man."

"How did you happen to work for Mr. Marlan?"

"I was in Frisco with a friend of mine. A painter, whom
I'd met hitch-hiking to California. I ran away, you see. He
took me to a party. Nils Drexel was there. The next day I got
a call to go to Mr. Marlan's suite at the Fairfax. He hired me
as a sort of secretary. I'm eternally grateful. It's just been
heaven."

"How old are you, Roddy?"

"Twenty."

I looked at his vapid eyes, his dough-like skin, his mad,
fluttering hands. I should have felt pity I suppose but I felt
only a sudden overwhelming revulsion. He was like a tired
little puppet repeating parrot-like phrases in a dreary emu-
lation of gaiety. There was no gaiety, no happiness, in those
eyes. There was something else, cold and empty as ice.

"Oh dear," he said. "I almost forgot what I started out to
do. I do hope I shall see you soon."

He smiled mechanically and started for the door. But before

he was halfway across the room the double doors opened and Drexel stood there, an expression of extreme annoyance on his Nordic face.

"Where have you been, MISTER Grayle! Mr. Marlan rang for you ten minutes ago!"

Grayle scuddled past Drexel into the next room with a look of venom.

Drexel said, "Mr. Marlan will be with you in a few minutes, Mr. Denby."

He disappeared back into the next room and I was alone again. Drink in hand I wandered about the room. On a small desk near the foyer door—a desk which was probably used during the day by some sort of a receptionist—I spotted an inter-office instrument. Casually, not really expecting anything, I pressed down the button and placed my ear near the sound box. To my astonishment, Marlan's voice came out of it. At first I thought he was indulging in some sort of monologue when I realized he was speaking to someone in the room with him, undoubtedly seated at a desk on which stood a replica of the sound box I was listening to.

I took a quick look at the doors. Both closed. I sat quickly at the desk and began to listen.

"...a great disappointment to me. Your report sounds like an itinerary made up by Cook's. He visits Lautrec's like any tourist and goes in the back room with a native whore."

A voice, fainter, further away from the sound box, said, "He has a peculiar way of slipping out of the picture. I cannot..."

The rest of what was said was undistinguishable. I gathered whoever spoke was pacing back and forth. The voice was familiar. But at first I couldn't place it.

"Fortunately for my interests," Marlan went on, "you are far from my only source of information. According to your report you have no idea where he was from the time he left Mrs. Fayne's party until he appeared at Lautrec's dive. And ·

then you leave, assuming your duties are finished for the night when he goes into the back room with the whore. What time was that?"

"Three o'clock."

I stiffened in surprise. The voice belonged to Berkeley. And for some reason he was lying. I left Lautrec's at two-thirty. Was he putting the hour at three in order to give himself an alibi for certain other activities in the vicinity of Siraud et Cie?

For a moment there was silence. Then Marlan went on smoothly, "Have you discovered for whom he works? Is he with the Russians? Or the others?"

"I doubt if he is with either."

"You doubt! You are not paid for theorizing. I want facts. Why did he have in his possession the Persian Cat? Is it a cover?"

"I need more time..."

"Time! This man is dangerous! I can use a man like that on my side. Or at least, pretend to. I believe he will put on an act for my benefit. He expects me to make an offer. He will pretend to accept. For his own purposes. He will believe himself very clever. We shall see."

There was a moment's pause. Then he went on, "Grayle. Take this down to Haussan immediately."

Quickly I snapped up the button and moved away from the desk. When Grayle came in from the next room I was busy examining a shelf of leather bound books on the other side of the room.

"I do hope we shall see you later, Mr. Denby," he said with a vacuous smile.

I turned to him with my blood freezing. He had heard what Marlan had said in the next room yet nothing showed on his face but simpering friendliness. I realized there was more than ice behind his wandering eyes. Not so simple as I'd thought. He tossed his head and went out into the foyer softly, closing the door behind him.

I thought, the vampire is ineffectual with the dawn. But dawn was still an hour away.

The double doors opened and Berkeley and Drexel came out. Berkeley stopped dead on the threshold, then turned angrily to Drexel.

"Why didn't you tell me he was waiting here!" Drexel shrugged elegantly.

"Hail Britannia," I said.

The Oxonian said, "Nuts," strode across the room and went out into the foyer banging the door behind him. Drexel said, "Mr. Marlan will see you now, Denby."

Said the spider to the fly, thought I. I followed him past the guards. We walked through a small room, like a room in Versailles, one of those perfect Louis Quinze rooms with everything but the ropes and the tourist signs, through more double doors into the inner sanctum.

Here there was none of the paraphernalia of the western business world. Candlelight flickered on oriental luxury. Near a window overlooking the garden a table was set for two. Marlan still in white tie and tails approached graciously, thanked me for coming, apologized for the unconventional hour and added, "My friends would not be surprised. You see my day is divided into three parts. The early evening is for pleasure, the remainder of the night I work. It is so wherever I go. I sleep during the day."

The vampire all right. I wondered if a spike through his heart would work at sunrise.

"The best of civilization is available only after sunset," he said.

"As an ex-soldier who saw most of the killing during the daylight hours, I am inclined to agree," I said.

He smiled as though I had said something witty and led the way to the table. Drexel had disappeared, apparently through one of the walls, or perhaps gone up in smoke from some Aladdin's lamp.

As we seated ourselves, I said, "I'm surprised that it has never occurred to you to be a theatrical impresario, Mr. Marlan. You have a delightful sense of the dramatic."

"Thank you. At least I assume you mean that as flattery. As a matter of fact, I am in a way comparable to an impresario. I back the newly formed Ballet de Continent, you know. It is to have its premiere in Buenos Aires in September."

"Ah yes. With Serge Lifar as leading dancer, I understand."

"Exactly." He gave me a bland look. "All that idiotic talk of Lifar's collaboration during the German occupation of Paris!" He went on to explain. "Professional jealousy. Gossip originated by infuriated rivals. He is a genius, the greatest since Nijinski. It is absurd to think that an artist has politics."

"I wouldn't know," I said. "Politics bore the hell out of me."

An Iranian servant appeared at my elbow and thrust some sort of an omelette before me. Marlan filled a long stemmed glass with an amber colored liquid and handed it to me. I didn't hesitate but sipped it immediately. His eyelids flickered with the faintest traces of humor.

"I am flattered by the way you drink without waiting, monsieur. Perhaps it is a new twist on good manners. These days, waiting for the host might imply a certain lack of faith."

"I can't imagine you stooping to the crudities of the Borgias," I said with more conviction than I felt. We were tearing aside the veils more quickly than I had anticipated.

"I like directness in others," he said. He sipped his wine. I noticed that his lips flinched away from the glass as though the touch of the solid material was unbearable to him.

"Good," I told him. "In that case we will not waste one another's time. Unless I am mistaken you believe I have come here hoping to get some sort of a business offer from you which I would accept for the purpose of spying on you. Correct?"

Slowly he put down the glass. I knew that I had floored him. However nothing showed on his face but polite surprise. After a moment he said in a puzzled manner, "It is true, Mr. Denby, that I have a certain taste for the dramatic, but I assure you that it is you who have a too highly developed sense of melodrama. I am a rich man with certain international interests. I must avail myself of information impossible to procure through the press, the embassies or ordinary channels of communication. But spying!" He laughed metallically. "Your experiences in the O.S.S. and with the Deuxième Bureau have apparently given you a distorted picture of ordinary business procedure."

I yawned. "Let's talk about the ballet, then."

The smile faded. For a moment his eyes were positively venomous. I thought of an old cobra coiling to strike. But he subsided and said, "Perhaps I am mistaken about you. It did occur to me that if I should make you an offer, your experience as a mercenary might not be the best to insure loyalty."

I waited, knowing I had gained a point. He was not too sure of himself now. I knew that, underneath, he was wondering whether I might not actually be of more use to him alive than dead. Just wondering. But it was a step forward. However, there was something else bothering him.

"Why did you come to Teheran," he asked.

Now was the time. I considered all the factors swiftly. I couldn't be sure how much he knew but was pretty certain it was almost everything. The way he had misled Berkeley. I was certain, for instance, he knew I had been standing on the balcony of Claire Fayne's room while he was there. And if he knew that much it was a safe guess that he knew far more.

My guess was that he knew almost everything except the

most important. Who my employers—my former employers—actually represented. The fact that I had tried to persuade Claire Fayne to go to Algiers might point to the true
nature of their interests. On the other hand, I felt strongly
that in Marlan's mind there existed a doubt. It might have
been a front to conceal my actual assignment, would be his
reasoning.

I leaned back in my chair, took another sip of wine and
said, "I don't know whether or not you can understand this,
Mr. Marlan, but I'm going to be frank with you."

Almost immediately I regretted that approach. He was
experienced enough to know that when a man says "I'm going to be frank with you" his intentions are anything but
candid. Quickly I fought for lost territory.

"There was a time," I began, "when I was a shiny-eyed
kid with all the clichés at my command..."

"What sort of clichés?"

"The crusade for democracy, for instance."

"I do hope, Mr. Denby, that you haven't lost faith in the
splendid form of government your country practices." His
tone was openly cynical, his eyes so derisive I needed all the
will power at my command not to turn over the table and
beat the hell out of him. Instead I felt myself grinning.

"The end of the war changed that. You see before you a
man without a country. My national flag is the dollar or the
franc or the lira, and a high rate of exchange. I got a damn
good price from the Deuxième for the little job I did for
them. That was my only interest. I'm getting a helluva good
fee for the job I'm on now. Too good to give up without the
assurance of a better offer."

"You still haven't told me whom you represent."

"And I won't tell you, Mr. Marlan, until I know your
price."

He laughed dryly. "You are being clever, but not clever
enough."

"Have it your way, then."

I pushed back my plate and stood and said pleasantly, "It's been amusing, but I'm afraid we are wasting time. I could use some sleep."

He let me get almost to the door before he said sharply, "Just a minute."

I turned, polite but bored.

"I'm going to give you a chance," he said. He was standing now and his face was tense. He'd left ballet talk far behind him. "But I warn you, Mr. Denby, lying will do you not the slightest bit of good. The first lie on your part would, I'm afraid, be most unfortunate for you."

"Depends on the size of the check," I said.

"Come back and sit down!" It was an order, snapped out in a truly Prussian manner. I took my time. He waited impatiently until I was seated. "You were born in Texas," he said, "you must know something about oil."

"Yes."

"I can fit a man of your peculiar experience into my organization. I'm willing to double whatever fee you now command."

"That's turkey," I said.

"Well?"

I lit a cigarette and looked thoughtful. "You've heard of the Raven Syndicate?"

His face was frankly skeptical. "You don't look Raven to me. Not with the setup you have. What are the French people doing in it?"

"They're hep to this underground business. I'm afraid that's where my trouble has been coming from. Some Persian no like. Some Persian get tough. Some of my people get hurt."

"What does Raven want?"

"Wants to know what the hell's going on up in the desert."

The worried look left his face. "Waste of time, my boy.

Geologists have been all over that desert three times. I've seen the reports. I would suggest that you radio Ed Hartley and the rest of the Raven boys that the output they seek is not in this country at all."

"Can do."

"You will sever any connection with these French people immediately."

"Yes."

"I will assume then that from this moment you are in my employ?"

"Yes."

"Drexel will talk money with you."

"Good."

"It still puzzles me, Denby, a man of your ability getting mixed up with a cheap outfit like Raven."

"Their asking price was not too cheap."

He stood and began pacing back and forth. I couldn't tell whether or not he had swallowed the story about Raven or was only pretending to accept it. And I knew he was not finished with me yet.

"You'll like Iran," he said. "There is a good life here. You can live like a king. Under certain circumstances I am willing to do far more than double the fee paid you by Raven."

"I believe I know the circumstances."

"Oh?" His back was still to me.

"That I stay away from Claire Fayne."

He stopped pacing. He stood there very still. After a moment he turned. There was a half smile on his face. I hadn't expected that smile; something cold went dancing through my stomach.

"I'm afraid you do not understand me at all, Mr. Denby."

I stumbled on, lost, groping, unsure. "My tactics have been pretty crude in that direction. I find Mrs. Fayne very attractive but I assure you my real interest in her was purely business."

"Business?"

"I thought if I could attain her confidence I could get some useful information for Raven. I went back to her room and made an exhibition of myself..."

"Exhibition?" he said softly.

"I told her some wild west story of a man named Altmont who was supposed to be in trouble in Algiers. It was a mistake in character analysis on my part. As you know, she would have none of me."

The smile seemed painted on his face. He closed his eyes. "It is boring to be constantly misunderstood," he said.

I stopped talking then, waiting, suddenly anxious to be out of this room, yet waiting because I had no choice.

"Claire is a normal young woman," he said. "I have her interests very close to my heart. She has been lonely since Reggie's death. There is one role in her life I cannot, or let us say, do not choose to play. You see, my interest in you is not merely confined to business."

One part of my mind said, I know; but another part pushed the knowledge quickly down into the storeroom of the unconsciousness.

"Claire has a delightful sense of humor, you know," he continued. "She will be relieved to discover all this Altmont business was so much fantasy. And though the joke was crude, she will forgive you." His eyes were still closed. "You are both young and healthy."

Suddenly he stopped and opened his eyes. He looked like a patient coming out from the influence of a drug. "As for your staying away from Mrs. Fayne, it would be impertinent for me to give you any such instructions. As long as you are discreet, I do not care."

He moved to the wall and yanked at a tapestried bell-rope. "And now, you must be tired. I will have you shown to your room."

"My room!"

"I prefer that you remain in the house until our business relationship is more clearly defined."

"My luggage," I said lamely.

"I will have it fetched from the Provençal." The half smile was back on his face.

A servant appeared and Marlan spoke to him in Persian. I knew I was being dismissed. Deflated and feeling slightly ill, I started to follow the servant from the room.

Behind me the old man said softly, "Sometime before luncheon you will see Drexel and give to him the names of your former associates. The Frenchmen you say were also employed by Raven."

"Yes, sure," I said casually enough, but my heart skipped a beat.

I followed the servant out through the reception room into the hall, up a curving stairway and finally to a bedroom on the second floor. It all seemed strangely unreal. Even my despair. I thought of the expressions on the faces of Lautrec and Pinel when they heard I had moved into Marlan's house from the Provençal. I wondered how in hell I could warn them.

The room overlooking the patio was sumptuous. High ceiling, green tile, priceless rugs, a bed out of a London museum. I stood for a long time watching the fountain in the garden below until the water began to gleam with a soft pink light. Dawn was marching in from the brown hills. The dawn that Gaby would never see.

Chapter 10

My belief in Denby-the-smart-operator lasted until luncheon. My clothes arrived, as arranged for by Marlan, and at noon I had an interview with Drexel in which I gave him Gaby's name along with three entirely fictitious French names. He disregarded my creative work and concentrated on Gaby.

"She worked at Siraud et Cie?"

"Worked? Why past tense?"

"She's dead. It's all over the morning paper. But I guess I don't have to tell you that."

"Too bad," I said coolly. "She was a good lay." And I said a silent prayer, asking her to forgive me.

"Why did you kill her," he asked curiously.

I yawned. "Don't be dumb, Drexel old boy. I don't go around killing little girls. She was doing a minor job for me. Strictly small potatoes. Practically clerical work. Looks to me like some Persian papa played too rough."

"She did not come into this country with the express purpose of doing business for Raven?"

"Good God, no. I picked her up at the Excelsior Cinema. Thought she might be useful for some wearisome detail work. I guess you know the sort of detail I mean. That's a two syllable word, brother. It was convenient to have her put on the payroll."

"And these others?"

I shrugged. "You may have trouble digging them up," I said.

"I don't doubt that!"

His irony didn't disturb me too much.

"That's all for now. Mr. Marlan is having guests to lunch. You are expected to circulate."

"That doesn't sound like manual labor."

My brains must have been still at the bottom of one of last night's glasses. Otherwise the abruptness of the interview would have wised me up. As it was, too sure of myself, certain that my only immediate worry was contacting Pinel, I slicked up for luncheon and walked out to the swimming pool in a large sunken garden behind the house where the "informal" affair was to take place.

The pool, an enormous blue tile figure eight, was set half way down the garden, on the edge of a small slope which looked out over the plain and the distant city. On one side beneath a scarlet canopy, long tables were set with food and drink and surrounding it were colorful outdoor chairs and tables. Except for the sprinkling of Persians (men only, of course) the scene might have been set in Beverly Hills. Some young people were playing about the pool shouting at one another in French and English, and forty or fifty people ranging from dowagers in enormous picture hats to rather seedy looking under-secretaries sat about in groups, eating, drinking and carrying on their eternal chatter where they had left off the previous night at Mrs. Fayne's soiree. Grayle, a slim dream in gray flannel, flitted about from group to group, concentrating on the more formidable looking dowagers. Marlan, in glistening white, held court at the far side of the pool. Claire Fayne sat half round the pool, chic and cool looking in a simple brown linen dress, talking with three youngish men, two of them European, and one, despite his London suit, obviously a Persian.

The men talked and smiled, preening themselves like male sparrows, doing their duty towards acceptable social flirtation with what was obviously more than lip service. Her face was half turned from me and she was smiling up at them but even in the distance she looked remote and her eyes seemed to be gazing at some point beyond the men.

Marlan caught my eye and beckoned. I grabbed a drink from the buffet and went to him aware of many curious eyes turned my way. All except Claire Fayne. She seemed oblivious of my existence. The group around Marlan parted. A man who had been standing almost directly in front of Marlan turned to face me. It was Pinel. Somehow I kept on moving, kept on smiling, kept the shock from my face.

Marlan was staring at me, the corners of his mouth turned up in a half smile.

"M. Durand, I want to have you meet Mr. Denby, who has only recently consented to be an associate of mine."

The derision was velvet. My self confidence was vanishing fast. I noticed a girl who had just leaped from the high-dive, gliding up to the surface of the pool in a long slant, hands straight down at her sides, for all the world like some rigid fish.

Pinel bowed. His eyes betrayed not the faintest sign of recognition. "Enchanté," he said.

"M. Durand is on a world tour," Marlan said. "It sounds almost like the good old days, doesn't it? Instead of the United Nations, we might discuss lion hunting in Kenya or the tea dancing at Raffles. M. Peneux, the French consul, was kind enough to bring him."

Marlan seemed to be in good humor. If he had any suspicion as to Pinel's real identity he was doing an excellent job of concealment. To my embarrassment he treated me like a favorite.

"Mr. Denby has just joined my staff," he explained. "I have great hopes for his future."

Pinel lifted his glass. "To Mr. Denby's future." There was no irony in his voice. His eyes were politely indifferent.

"M. Durand and I have been gossiping about the murder," Marlan said. The others had drifted away, only Pinel and I were left at his side.

"Murder?"

"A French girl was found with her neck broken in the Rue Revjed last night, or rather in the early hours of the morning. So far it seems to be one of those intriguing crimes without apparent motivation."

"Yes, I know about it," I said.

"Indeed?" Pinel's voice was sharp.

"Mr. Drexel, Mr. Marlan's secretary, was just telling me about it. It's in the papers, you know."

"Undoubtedly a *crime passionale*," Pinel said after a minute.

"This climate breeds that sort of Victorian nonsense."

Marlan was watching me curiously. "The girl. She couldn't by any chance be one of the French persons you spoke about last night, Denby."

I felt the color creeping up my face. I didn't dare look at Pinel. "Drexel and I just discussed it," I said shortly.

"Ah, then I was right. No matter. We won't discuss it now."

I looked furtively at Pinel. He was carefully avoiding my eyes. I knew he must be desperate to have come out in the open like this. I prayed that he realized my apparent attachment to Marlan was in his own interests. But after the last business from Marlan about "the French persons we discussed," I didn't hold out much hope.

"Whoever committed such a brutal crime will be punished, I have no doubt," Pinel said. For the first time he looked at me. A direct look, deadly and unmistakable. Then he turned back to Marlan, bowed, excused himself and wandered off to the buffet.

"Now I wonder whom *he's* working for," Marlan said.

I laughed. "Aren't there any true tourists in this party, Mr. Marlan?"

He giggled appreciatively. It was his kind of humor. "I should be very much surprised if there were." He was in a good mood. "Sit down, my boy. I must have this Durand person investigated."

He fitted a cigarette into his holder and I held the light for him. Then he leaned back in the wicker chair and looked across the crowd at Claire. I followed his glance. She was still half turned from us, her face tilted up to the three men.

"I have collected many jewels in my life," Marlan said after a moment, "but I have never been really a very avid collector. A jewel comes to one in its completed state, there is no chance to improve upon it, to watch it blossom, to mold it and to approach the day when perfection is of one's own making."

"But then," I said carefully, "the sort of object it would give you pleasure to collect has its drawbacks."

"In what way?"

"There is always the danger that, once the state of perfection has been attained, someone else will possess it."

His face turned to me. The smile was there. The smile he had worn the previous night. I had the impression of a crack appearing on the surface, a crack through which one had a faint glimpse into dark, pathological depths.

"No," he said quietly, "you see it could only be touched in turn by another of my possessions."

I tried quickly to retreat by changing the subject but he interrupted me sharply.

"I wish Claire to be married."

I took a gulp of the drink.

"Once I thought I had found the right man for her. A man I thought I could manage. It turned out to be a ghastly mistake. An almost irrevocable one. Almost, but not quite. Fortunately, it did not end in disaster. Next time there must be no such mistake."

I fought down an impulse to run and even managed to look interested.

"You are a man of action, Denby," he said. "You are dangerous. But so is a wild animal before it is trained. I am not a man of action. I'm the planner, the thinker. In a way we complement one another." He laughed lightly. "I suppose I might say that a man of your type is my fulfillment. If you are sympathetic and learn complete loyalty, you can go far. Fortunately your needs from women are, I imagine, fairly elemental. I should have no wish to trespass on your territory and you must never trespass on mine. Do we understand one another?"

The picture that rose instantaneously to my mind was of a marriage bed. I almost felt Marlan entering my body, clutching vicariously at the woman amid the rumpled sheets. Suddenly the drink tasted like sewer water.

"Well?"

All about us people were laughing and flirting. There was the constant clinking sound of glass and silver on plate in the clear, hot air. The young people moved about the pool like lazy seals. Hands reached up and over the tiled brink for drinks. A pale blonde, minus a bathing cap, hair strewn about her shoulders like white silk, floated about the pool on a rubber swan.

Marlan was waiting.

"I think perhaps I understand," I managed to say.

"I'm sure you do." His voice was edged low with a suggestion of restrained excitement. "Of course I'm taking a chance on you, Denby. I'll be frank to admit that I was prepared to trick you, believing that your offer to work for me was merely a ruse. But somehow I have more faith in your good sense. And, almost complete faith in what you will do for money."

"Thanks," I said dryly. I felt as though slime were dripping from my lips.

And then, as I lifted my head from the glass, I saw Drexel making his way through the crowd. Without any plausible mental reaction I knew instantly that something had gone wrong. His face was set towards Marlan and he brushed aside the guests as though they were stage props. Electricity seemed to have entered my spinal column.

"What's wrong, my boy?" Marlan asked.

"I don't know," I said, "yet."

Chapter II

"Well?" Marlan seemed annoyed by Drexel's intrusion.

"I'm sorry, Mr. Marlan, but this is urgent." Drexel's voice was ominous.

"Speak up."

Instead of answering, Drexel looked at me significantly. I got to my feet.

"No, stay here, Denby. You're one of the family now. Might as well begin to share our secrets."

Obviously, Drexel didn't agree. "I must speak with you alone, Mr. Marlan."

The moments of silence seemed endless. The voices about me were like the chirping birds in the noonday sun. Marlan's small eyes were fixed on Drexel. He said, "If you don't mind, Denby..." He seemed slightly bored.

"I must speak to Mrs. Fayne," I said, and left them. They were silent until I was out of earshot. I felt as though an icicle were boring into the small of my back.

And there was not much warmth in the picture before me. Claire Fayne was watching my approach with a cold smile. She offered me her hand in an exaggerated manner that was a travesty on friendliness.

"How delightful!" She introduced me to the three gentlemen. I froze them out quickly. Resentfully they drifted off. She seemed indifferent as I sat beside her.

"I have a membership card," I said.

"I don't doubt it!" Her voice was edged with contempt.

Surreptitiously, I glanced toward Marlan and Drexel.

"I have a feeling though that it's only an associate membership. I'm afraid I'm about to be drummed out of the regiment."

"How sad for you," she said mockingly. "However, as

long as you have fulfilled Edmund's purpose...?"

"What do you mean?"

Only her eyes betrayed her anger. "Don't be dull! Which one of you made up that fairy tale about Altmont? You or Edmund?"

"I wasn't working for Marlan last night."

She laughed. "You had about as much finesse as a cockney private detective attempting to frame a convent-bred debutante. I never went to a convent, and I'm hardly a debutante."

"You don't honestly believe that Marlan..."

"I must have a talk with Edmund. That sort of thing is really too crude for him." She smiled sweetly. "I don't like my bedroom cluttered up with his... his things."

"Listen, Claire. I've been playing both ends against the middle. It was a mistake. The ends are about to close up like an accordion, and unless I get out?"

She yawned. "I think you're exactly where you belong."

"I'm not working for anybody now but myself. Please believe me. Let me take you home."

She looked at me. Her eyes were hard but in them was a speculative quality I had not noticed before. And then she looked beyond me and suddenly the cynical disbelief vanished and in its place there was doubt.

"What's happening," she said.

There were little wisps of panic around the edges of her voice. I turned. Haussan, the chauffeur, was making his way through the crowd to Marlan's side. I knew I had to play fast.

"I'm getting out," I said. "I'll telephone you at four."

"How terribly kind of you. My servants will be instructed to inform you I'm not at home."

"Think it over," I said.

Suddenly her fingers tightened about mine and she said in a low voice, "If it's really true, if you are about to be 'at liberty,' call me. You interest me as a type. You're the most unspeakable heel I've ever met."

I bowed, smiled and turned. Haussan was at Marlan's side now, bending over his master, listening. All the time his eyes were on me.

"So long, Texas," I said over my shoulder. I went to the buffet and got myself a plate of food, trying to look as though I had no place to go. A servant tapped me on the shoulder. "Pardon, monsieur, M. Marlan wish to see you."

"Thank you."

Not much sand left in the top of the hour glass. Marlan was watching me, his face set as ivory. Drexel was still there with Haussan. They were a little tableau of three, all of them watching me. I waved and smiled as though to say, "be right there, old boy," and began to search the crowd for Pinel. I found him standing under the far end of the canopy, alone, calmly concentrating on a lobster salad. I got close to him and said out of the corner of my mouth, "Something's gone wrong. There's going to be trouble. I think Marlan has you spotted."

He went on eating for a moment then said, "Even Marlan wouldn't attempt murder before half of Teheran."

"This isn't charades."

"Is that what you said to Gaby?" His voice was almost gentle.

"You're wrong, Pinel." I stopped as he moved away. I knew there was no use following him. I made my way casually to the fringe of the crowd and then started quickly up the path towards the house. When I looked back I saw that Haussan had left Marlan's side and was coming after me. I began to move faster and when I got behind a clipped hedge, began to run.

The tiled arcade of the main house was deserted. All the doors opening off it were closed tight. I dropped the plate and its contents into a large blue vase. It made an echoing clatter. All the way around the patio I passed no one but by the time I reached the front entrance I could hear Haussan there, coming swiftly across the tiles. I hurtled out onto the front terrace. A footman jumped to attention. There was a long line of limousines and sport cars down the curving drive. Chauffeurs stood about in small groups, smoking and chattering.

The footman came forward questioningly. I waved him aside. "I'm walking," I said. But of course I was running. I got quickly around on the other side of the cars and began to hurry towards the distant gates.

Behind me, someone shouted. I sprinted. The lions guarding the gates were like dread figures which seemed to recede instead of coming closer. Someone was scurrying down the gravel alongside the cars. The lions were closer now. In another moment I would be through them and out on the main road to Teheran.

And then, to my consternation, the great iron gates began slowly to swing shut.

Even at a distance, while still running, I swung out my hands to prevent their inexorable movement. I strained every muscle in the forward motion; my lungs were bursting. The grill work inched inwards. I was almost there now. The margin of freedom was only a yard. With a final burst of speed I hurtled through the opening and the gates clanged to behind me.

Two men leaped out from behind the hedges and grabbed me. I struck out blindly. My fist found something soft. Someone cursed, and then there were more men, too many men and there was no use fighting.

I relaxed. The hands were all over me. I saw the car in the dusty road. And then I realized these were not Marlan's men, they were the Teheran police.

Berkeley stepped out of the car. "That's your man," he said.

Haussan was back behind the gates, a wide grin on his ugly face. The policemen shoved me towards the black touring car.

"What's all this about?" I asked, in the how-dare-youto-an-American-citizen tone of voice. I made no impression.

"Just a formality," Berkeley said. "They want you to go to the police house for some questioning."

"I like their formal manners," I said. I was pushed firmly into the rear of the car and Berkeley got in beside me and I was thinking, it's bad but not as bad as it would be behind those gates.

We started down the long dusty road towards the city. Just before we reached the first gate Berkeley leaned forward and said something to the driver. Berkeley settled and offered me a cigarette. I accepted. No one spoke. We made our way through the crowded back streets and to my surprise finally drew up before the Provençal.

"Since when has this dump become the police house?" I asked.

"All in good time," Berkeley said. "As you can see, the police and I are on very friendly terms. First we will have a drink in my room."

The uniformed policeman stayed in the car but two plainclothes men followed us into the lobby, shared the elevator with us and stood in the hall outside Berkeley's room as we entered. Berkeley shut the door and got out a bottle of scotch.

"It's a good bluff," I said. "But it won't work. The police don't dare arrest me because they have no evidence. I suppose your job is to get that evidence the smooth way."

"I owe you a drink, old man," he said.

"You also owe me a Persian Cat," I said. He disregarded this.

I took the drink and said, "What's the gimmick?"

"You've probably read the papers. A woman has been murdered. Her name was Gaby Siraud. I'm a curious sort of bloke. I want to know why she was murdered."

"Never heard of her," I said sarcastically.

He laughed. "You were seen leaving the office of Siraud et Cie a few minutes before the body was discovered."

"What were you doing there?"

His eyebrows went up. "I? Oh no, old chap, really no. In fact, I didn't get my information until an hour ago."

"And you telephoned Marlan and talked to Drexel?"

"Let's not waste time on the sordid details. What I want from you, Denby, is talk. Talk that makes sense. Otherwise, you'll have to take your chances with the local police."

"I don't get it," I said. "You work for Marlan and the British Government and you can square things with the local police."

"It's a trick that takes years to learn."

"Why the hell are you so fascinated with me?"

"Somebody gave you a bum steer with that Persian Cat, Denby. It's a legitimate organization but there are leaks in it. I knew you were in town ten minutes after the customs man spotted you. I know you went to see someone at Siraud and I also know Siraud works with certain undercover groups. So does Lautrec. I haven't been in this town for twenty years for nothing. I did slip up in one thing, though. I thought you were finished for the night when I saw you follow the dancing girl into the back room at Lautrec's. I went to Marlan's for a nightcap. I didn't hear about your visit to Siraud's office after you left Lautrec until an hour ago."

"And you told the cops where to look."

"Yes. But not with too much emphasis on your possible guilt. I don't want to tie you up decisively until I have to. Now then, use your head, Denby. I've got to know what you're doing here."

"I've already told Marlan. I'm here for the Raven syndicate."

He laughed. "You had Marlan almost believing that last night. He changed his mind less than an hour ago. At least, he will have changed his mind if Drexel has had a chance to talk with him."

"He has."

"I happen to know the whole Raven setup here, old boy. You don't fit into it anywhere. Come clean. Then you can drink up and we'll have another and I'll tell the local boy guides to go home."

"And the alternative?"

"The police. Marlan. Either choice will not be pleasant for you."

"It doesn't sound pleasant," I said.

He was smiling as I hurled my glass into his face. He didn't have time to stop smiling before I followed up with a fist right into the middle of his sallow face. But he'd stopped smiling by the time my knee came up.

I lugged him into the bathroom, dumped him in the tub and stood there for a moment figuring out a graceful exit. Then I walked through the bedroom to the hall door, opened it and beckoned urgently and mysteriously to the two Mack Sennett cops standing in the hall. They came running, all frowns and uncertain glances at one another. I ushered them past me, pointed tragically at the bathroom door and, as they stepped over the threshold like two rabbits into a trap, slammed the hall door with me on the outside and began to run like hell.

I was half way down the service stairs before bedlam broke loose. The entire hotel seemed alive with shouts and curses. I reached a lower hall, ran head on through a swing door into a kitchen where an evil-looking cook and two or three employees who looked like candidates for a leper colony were giving imitations of a human-statue act symbolizing frozen surprise, and on out into a garbage-filled alley inhabited by a flock of goats. Even in my understandable haste

I made a mental note, as I flew across the kitchen, never to take another meal at the Provençal.

I decided against the street entrance to the alley and, instead, vaulted a low stone wall into the courtyard of a native hotel. There were more goats here and some interesting smells, but finding myself with a singular lack of tourist curiosity at the moment, I dashed across the yard, clambered over another wall into a narrow dark alley and finally made an undignified exit into one of the narrow streets behind the hotel.

After that it was tag all the way with oriental sound effects. I began to feel like Eliza without a little Eva to induce sympathy. Several times the human bloodhounds were damned near but finally, against Mr. Coward's advice pertaining to the white man's activity in the noonday sun, I left the sound of what appeared to be half the native population baying in the distance. I slowed down to a respectable slouch. I was in a native bazaar or souk. I was wetter than I could possibly have been in Marlan's swimming pool.

I puttered about the stalls trying to look like a tourist and succeeding I suppose, because I must have appeared quite demented. I bought a shawl that looked more Spanish than Persian. I thought of homes in the mid-west where uprights are bought with the sole purpose of placing them under such shawls. And then I began to have practical shopping ideas.

Twenty minutes later I emerged from the rear of one of the stalls looking like a faded print of a Valentino movie. If any of the natives who had seen me enter the stall in a white linen suit only to come out looking like something headed for the Beaux Arts Ball were surprised, they gave no hint of it. In fact before I left the souk I began to feel almost at home in the fez and burnoose. It's true that as I emerged into one of the winding streets a small child ran from me with horror in its dark eyes and a donkey veered sharply to the left as I passed, but these incidents were too unimportant to destroy my newly acquired self-confidence. I thought, if Lawrence of Arabia could do it, Denby of Iran can certainly give him a close race.

In one of the cafes off the Maden, I found a telephone. I told the servant at Mrs. Fayne's to tell her Mr. Dallas was phoning. In a moment she came on.

"Hello, darling," I said, "I thought you were not going to be at home."

"It's an off day," she said. "Things are dull. I'm curious."

"Let me come and tell you a tale out of the *Thousand and One Nights*."

"You're no Scherezade," she said.

"Luckily for you, no. But at the moment I'm giving a good imitation of some distant male relative. Have you ever worn a burnoose?"

"Really," she said, "I think you're not only crooked, immoral and dangerous, but also mad."

"I can't just walk in on you. Marlan's playboys wouldn't like it."

There was a long silence and then she said, "I'll pick you up in my car. Where are you?"

"Come down to the Maden and turn off into the Rue D'ar. I'll hop on as you turn the corner."

"Remember," she said. "It's just because I'm bored to tears."

"Oh sure." I hung up and stood in the small back room. It was possible of course that the only car that would come for me would be Marlan's black Rolls or something belonging to the police, but I doubted it. I suspected that she would play ball for her own reasons. Curiosity, power-drive, or maybe that she hoped I might be a satisfactory "Captain of the Guards."

I went to the appointed corner and tried to look as though I were waiting for a passing camel, ready to run at the first sign of a double cross. But my hunch was right. In ten min-

utes she came sailing around the corner in a Packard con-
vertible and slowed down along the curb. I hopped into the
rear and ducked down.

"Just pretend I'm groceries until we're home," I said.
"Don't talk."

She obeyed. After a while I realized we were turning into
the driveway of her house. In the daylight I was even more
impressed with its charming architecture than I had been
the night of the party. It was a pleasant contrast to Marlan's
palace.

"Pull down the door handle so that you'll be ready to jump
when I give you the word," she said. "And wait behind the
bushes for further developments."

I put my hand on the handle. Just before I jumped I said,
"That's nice perfume you use." Then I tumbled out into the
azaleas and crawled back among them until I was up against
the wall.

Chapter 12

The cocktail shaker was half empty. It stood on one of the
small gilt tables in her bedroom. So far she had made no in-
timation that a bedroom was anything more than a sub-
terfuge for a drawing room. She managed to keep half the
room between us.

I poured the remnants of the shaker into our glasses.

"You realize, of course, that you are now my prisoner?"

"Sweet captivity!" I said.

She yawned. "Don't waste your energy on that sort of
thing. I mean business."

"Let's hope it's..."

"No. I brought you back here because I must know certain
facts. I'm getting damned fed up with all this Aladdin and
the Lamp stuff."

"What's in it for you?"

"You said at luncheon you had been playing both ends against the middle only to find yourself caught in a squeeze play. I gather that you meant you had been working for both Edmund and someone else. I gather also that it had nothing to do with—how shall I put it?—business ethics?"

"That's good enough."

"In other words, that you could be had for a price."

"Smart girl," I said.

Her eyes were contemptuous but she went on in that hard, matter-of-fact voice. "Very well. Your double dealing seems to have landed you on a spot where further employment is going to be difficult here in Teheran. Apparently you won't get references from either of your former employers. You will, in other words, find yourself on the beach or in jail."

"That's what I like about American women. Their sentimentality."

"Now then. I'm offering you employment, Mr. Denby."

I sat on the chaise longue and finished off the cocktail in a gulp.

"I hope it means night work," I said.

"Definitely not." Her voice was sharp. "I can't pay what Edmund offered but then I'm in a good bargaining position. You either accept my salary or else I'll let Edmund or the police discuss it with you."

"What's the price?"

"Three thousand dollars. Enough to get you far enough away from Teheran so that you may have at least a prospect of a healthy future."

I pretended to be considering it. All the time I was wondering what this new angle meant. I thought perhaps Marlan thought I might spill the beans on my real purpose in coming to Teheran, if I believed Claire Fayne was actually engaging me for undercover work of her own. Her next words practically convinced me.

"What do you know about the death of the French girl?"

"No spika da Eenglish," I said insolently.

She shrugged impatiently. I noticed two little worry lines forming a V above her eyes. I thought, baby, you won't have to worry about anything by the time I'm finished with you.

"Do you want the job or not?"

"What does it entail?"

"Don't tell me you're going fastidious on me."

"I like to know what I'm being hired for. I'm the old-fashioned type of employee."

She put her empty glass aside and said, "I want you to find out why Edmund has put spies on me. I want you to find out exactly what he is up to."

For a moment I had to admire her. She made it sound so convincing. "Up to in what way?"

She looked away from me. "I used to trust Edmund implicitly. I believed everything he told me. He was like a father to me in a way. But it's like dreaming about being in some lovely place and then having the dream suddenly change into a nightmare. This may sound idiotic to you, but..."

Her hands were clasped tightly together in her lap. She looked furtively at the half-open window. I thought, she is putting up a damned good act.

"I'm afraid," she said simply.

"Texas girls don't scare easy," I said.

"Oh it's not for myself." A note of despair entered her voice. "If what I suspect is true I'm finished anyway. I'd be about as useful as a snowball in hell. No, it's not for me..."

And then, in the midst of her imitation of Katherine Cornell, and as though in answer to the question in my mind the hall door began to inch open. I jumped to my feet and turned, ready for almost anything.

But I wasn't prepared for what actually came into the room. It was a boy, no more than ten years old, a thin, little fellow in immaculate white, with a serious face and great blue eyes.

He stopped uncertainly just inside the door and glared at me. "You leave my mother alone!" he said.

"Charles!" She was across the room in a moment, leading him to me, his hand clasped tightly, protectively rather than in fear, in hers. "Darling," she went on, "Mr. Denby is a friend of mine. He is from America."

Despite the fact that the word American had obviously made a profound impression, he didn't relent altogether.

"Are you a friend of my mother's?" he asked.

"Yes, Charlie."

"Charles," he said. "Not Charlie." His eyes were fixed on my face with an intensity that was, to say the least, uncomfortable.

"Okay, Charles. Sorry."

"Women can be fooled easy," he said. "Ali knows that."

Claire Fayne had closed the door to the hall. Her manner had changed completely. There was a kind of fierce protective quality in her manner with the boy that made me think of a lioness with her cub and her eyes, when she looked at me now, were full of hostility. They seemed to be saying, this boy will be a man you can never hope to be.

"Where in America?" the boy asked. He hadn't come closer to me but stood his ground by his mother's side.

"I come from Dallas," I said. "That's in Texas."

"I know that," he said, putting me in my place. "But we're going to live in Connecticut. There are cows there. We're going to go in an airplane and we won't have to see Uncle Edmund again."

"Sh-h, Charles, you promised not to say that."

"But you said he was a friend, mother."

"Now darling. Mr. Denby and I have some business to discuss. I'll take you back to Morja."

"I don't have to be taken back." He bowed to me and there was something like adult irony in his voice when he said, "Good-bye, sir. I hope my mother is right. I mean, having a friend."

"Tomorrow I'll tell you all about Connecticut," I said. "It's one of my favorite places."

Claire Fayne went out into the hall with him. Quickly I began to fix another drink. To hell with that crap, I thought. It's something out of her bag of tricks. I'd passed the age where I dissolved into syrup at the sight of a mother-and-child.

When she came back I said, "Why have you been keeping this from me?"

"Let's not discuss it." Her voice was cold.

"Reggie?"

"I'm afraid so."

I gave her a quick look. *"Afraid?"*

"Nice for the kid, having a traitor for a father."

I slowly put down my glass. "You don't really believe that?"

"Oh God! I don't know what to believe any more. The world seems full of liars and murderers. What a horrible world to hand my son."

I sat on the chaise longue watching her closely. I began to feel uneasy. Somehow she was no longer like Dorothy. Whether or not it was a performance, she was damned effective.

"Claire."

She came across the room to me and flung herself down beside me. "I'm a damned fool," she sobbed. "Maybe it's because you look like Reggie, I don't know. I need help badly. I know you should be the last one in the world I should trust, but somehow..."

I drew her to me. For a moment I felt like Sir Galahad. But the perfume brought me back. I remembered Gaby.

"Of course you can trust me, Claire," I said. And all the time I was thinking of what she would look like falling before a firing squad.

Chapter 13

The bedroom was a small one on the third floor facing the front lawn and gates. After she had left me, there was a knock on the door and when I opened it the servant I had seen the night of Mrs. Fayne's party in the library came in. He had a dinner tray which he deposited on a small table near the window. Then quietly from under his robe he took the Persian Cat and placed it on top of the commode. His face was without expression. I thought, everyone seems to have one of those things but me. I remembered Berkeley had told me the customs inspector had reported to someone who, in turn, had tipped off British Intelligence.

"I suppose, Ali," I said, "you've already reported my presence in this house?"

"No," he said, "not yet."

"But you will have to make a report?"

His eyes were inscrutable. "Not if you request otherwise."

"I do. I'm in great danger, Ali."

"Of that I am aware." There was just the suggestion of a smile on his lips. "I will have fresh clothes for you tomorrow."

"Thank you." There wasn't any more to be said. I had to play it that way. After he left I had my dinner and settled down to a book. Claire had a dinner engagement at the British Embassy but she'd said she would stop in after she returned. The cigarette butts began to collect in the ashtray at my side as darkness fell. I was still fairly certain that Claire Fayne was playing a smart game, playing scared of Marlan in the hope that I would divulge my real purpose in being in Teheran. And I thought the trick of pulling the kid on me was about the lowest she could go. But all the same I could not account for the vague feeling of dissatisfaction. There was something wrong here. Was it barely possible that...?

I straightened up as there was a faint knock on the door. Cautiously I opened it. Charles stood there in his pyjamas.

"May I come in?"

I stepped aside. "Glad to have company," I said.

When I had shut the door he turned to me in a businesslike way. "There are some things it's better not to discuss in front of women," he said.

"Absolutely right," I said. "Sit down."

He sat opposite me. "I'm supposed to be asleep," he said. And then, as though this were too childish a note, he got businesslike again. "Who are you hiding from, Mr. Denby?"

"There are some things I have to find out, Charles." Then I added, "about some people who have not been so good."

"It's about him," he said.

"Who?"

"I used to have to call him Uncle Edmund. But mother says I don't have to if I don't want to now. I hate him."

"Why do you hate him, Charles?"

"Because my mother is afraid of him."

I lit a cigarette and said, "Who told you to come and tell me this, kid?"

He looked puzzled. "No one told me. They wouldn't like it if they knew. He makes my mother cry. She doesn't know that I saw her crying. I was hiding in her bedroom and she was all alone. And she was crying. People from America are good. You will help her."

"Did you always dislike Mr. Marlan?" I said. I was getting damned confused. The kid was on the level. At least he believed what he said.

"I don't remember much before," he said. "I was just a boy then. In France. And my father died and we went away. Mother cried a lot and I knew Uncle... he said bad things about my father."

"Listen, kid," I said. "Don't ever let anyone tell you different. Your father was a great man, a hero."

It was as though I had handed him the sun. His head went up. His lower lip trembled but there were no tears. He said nothing. I felt a lump in my throat and walked to the window.

After a moment, he said, "I knew it. I knew it all the time!" He lowered his voice and told me, "Uncle! Him! He's bad. He makes her cry. If you're a friend you'll help us go away. You'll take us away!"

The depression that came over me made me almost physically sick. I was going to take her away all right, but not in the way this kid thought.

"I've got to go now," he said. "I feel better with you here." He walked to the door, straight as a soldier, self-sufficient, independent, carrying his secret load of sorrow like a man. With one hand on the knob, he turned again and said, "I wouldn't have to ask you to help, only you see I'm not big enough yet."

"Listen, Charles..." I began.

"Charlie," he said. He smiled for the first time. "After what you said about my pop, I know you're okay. There's no one else I let call me Charlie except Ali."

"Soon you'll be back in America," I said.

"I never was there," he said. "I know all about it though. Mother told me and read from books. There are lots of kids my age going to the same school and you play baseball, and..."

"You're damned right you do!"

"What's wrong, Mr. Denby!" He gave me a worried look.

"Get to bed," I said harshly, "it's late."

After he had gone, softly closing the door behind him, I went to the window and stood there for a long time staring out at the lights of Teheran. I thought, that's the whole world for a kid like that. A world of liars and murderers. And then I realized I was thinking her words.

I began pacing back and forth for after a while I began on the bottle of scotch Ali had left for me. By the time Claire Fayne came in just before midnight I was well on my way towards a lost weekend. She looked very pale but unbelievably beautiful in a black dinner dress. She refused a drink and sat on the edge of the bed, subtly and inexplicably creating a platonic atmosphere. She seemed wrought up and jittery.

"How was the party?"

"God," she said, looking at me strangely.

"What's wrong?"

"Your name was brought up by my dinner partner. An attaché at the American Embassy."

"Oh?"

"He saw you coming out of the Provençal day before yesterday but you got away before he could reach you. He's been trying to get in touch with you ever since. His name is Bill Meaghan."

My hand froze on the glass. "Meaghan here in Teheran. The last time I saw him..."

"Exactly. He was a buddy of yours in the O.S.S. He seems to think you are practically God."

"Even the gods fall," I said.

"Gil," she said. "I don't believe you're a cynical mercenary. Not after what he said."

"He hasn't seen me in four years. Times change." I waited for the inevitable question. And I knew the answer would be relayed quickly to Marlan.

But to my surprise she said instead, "How much would it cost to charter a plane, for a trip to Cairo?"

Through the whisky fumes I put my guard up. "Why?"

"I want out, Gil. I want to get away. I want to take Charles back to the States."

I hid my astonishment. It was too neat. There was a trick in it somewhere. She couldn't be playing into our hands so easily. "I could arrange it," I said.

"Please, Gil. Do it as quickly as possible." She slipped a ring off her finger. "This is worth five thousand dollars. I'm low in cash but this should cover everything. My passport is in order."

"Why couldn't you just walk out on a regular airliner?"

"You don't know Edmund. He won't let me go if he suspects."

I noticed her fingers winding and unwinding and the stiff, unnatural posture of her body. But she had me puzzled. Not only was she falling into our hands, but offering to pay the price of her transportation to what looked from my position like her death. Once we got her aboard a plane we wouldn't touch earth until we had reached Algiers. I wondered if her motive was merely to get away from Marlan with rich loot and look for greener fields?

"What's it all about?" I asked.

"Charles," she said. "He's the only one who matters now."

I poured myself another drink, thinking, this is what I came here for. This is what Gaby wanted. Why the hell don't I feel set-up about it?

She watched me with a curious veiled expression. After a bit she said, "Gil. Please kiss me."

I didn't think she noticed my hesitation and perhaps if it had not been for the perfume there would not have been any hesitation, but after I had kissed her she looked up at me with a slight smile and said, "I see."

For once I was at a loss. Her mood confused me. She stood and walked to the window and turned. "Biography," she said.

"Why?"

"I want you to know."

For some reason I didn't want to hear. Now that she had asked me to arrange her departure from Teheran my only thought was to get the whole business over quickly. I didn't want to know any more about her. But I said nothing and after a moment she began.

"I was born in Dallas, you know."

"I guessed that when you said you had known a girl from Texas that first night in the library."

"What would you say my background had been?"

"Oh, an old man with oil derricks or a few thousand acres of cattle. Eastern finishing schools. Summers abroad."

She laughed. "Edmund deserves a great deal of credit. Actually my old man ran a grocery store down on Railroad Avenue."

"I know Railroad Avenue," I said.

"Sure you do. It's where you rich kids used to come slumming."

"I wasn't the 'slumming' type. I had some friends there. Pat Sullivan. Joe Vershevsky."

"My old man's store was three houses away from Vershevsky's shoe-shop."

"We must have passed many times in the street. It's a funny world. Never meeting."

"Maybe you were one of those wise guys in white flannels who used to come down to the corner of Railroad and First after school and give the Railroad Avenue girls the once over. Maybe you're one of the brats who got his face slapped!"

"I would have remembered if you had done the slapping!"

She ran her hands restlessly through her hair and half closed her eyes. "Funny," she said, "sometimes at a smart cocktail party at the Riviera or in London I would get the feeling that everything was a dream. I would lose the sense of assurance Edmund had so carefully built up in me. The Molyneux gown, the emeralds, the kind of silly chatter I had learned to spout, none of them helped. There I would sit feeling fourteen again, Claire Leary from Railroad Avenue, unhappy, eternally conscious of being on the wrong side of the tracks. I would turn to my dinner partner in a kind of panic, half expecting him to be winking at me like the boys on the corner of Railroad and First, half expecting him to leer and say 'hot stuff.'" She began to pace back and forth.

"I had something," she went on. "I had a good body and I read a lot and I was damned if I would sell out cheap. My mother died when I was ten and my old man was a drunk. I started working in a five and ten cent store when I was thirteen. And for five years until my old man was found dead in a gutter I fought off the small time wolves. I thought: not good enough—wait."

She gave me a defiant look. "You see, it wasn't that I objected to being a whore. Only I was making damned sure it would get me somewhere. Inside the core was pretty tough, Gil. It was tough before I was twelve.

"After my old man died I got a job at Marcus as a model. The offers began to go up. But I still held off. I was waiting for something else. Something good enough to put me in a position to spit in the faces of all the rich little brats who had snubbed me when I was a kid. And then, one day four of us, models from the store, went out to put on a fashion show at the country club. After the show we were allowed to mingle with the gentry. Mingling usually meant fighting off a gang of callow college kids or being polite to some cattle king who fancied himself as a man of the world. But this time it was different. Edmund Marlan was there as the guest of a well-known Dallas hostess and almost from the first I was aware of him watching me. Someone introduced us and he drew me aside, and talked to me almost for an hour. I was enchanted with him. It wasn't at all what I had expected. No subtle passes. No arch innuendoes. He talked to me about Europe and the people he knew and it was like listening to a fairy story. He was in the world I had always dreamed of. A world that would make even the most snobbish Dallas host-

ess look like a dairy-maid. And he seemed so gentle and understanding, Gil. Just before we parted he told me that he
admired my voice and casually, oh so casually, asked me if I
would like to join his staff as—of all things—a reader. Someone to read to him."

I laughed. "Bedtime stories?"

"Oh," she said, "I wasn't Little Red Riding Hood. I knew
what the score was. But even knowing I said 'yes' like a shot.
And I was wrong. There were no 'bedtime' stories. None at
all, Gil. There never were. He was like a father."

"My heart belongs to Daddy!"

"That's what everyone thought but it wasn't true. I joined
his staff next day and at the end of the week I left Dallas for
good. At first I didn't see much of him. I was just another
member of his secretarial staff. But I watched and began to
learn fast. Then one night in Vienna he took me to supper
and told me he had been watching me closely and had decided that he wanted to do something for me. When he asked
me if I would care to go on the stage or study singing I
thought I knew what 'doing something' for me meant. But
again I was wrong. When I asked why he was so interested
in doing something for me he said in the saddest voice in the
world, 'You look like my mother.' "

"The old silver cord," I said.

"Yes. I suppose so. But at the time I was touched. In a way
I began to think of him as the father I'd never had. Well,
anyway, I couldn't sing and I couldn't act, but I could wear
clothes and was quick to pick up the manners of any milieu
in which we moved. I have an acquisitive nature, like a
sponge. He began to take me around to parties. I knew people
were talking but I didn't give a damn and as for Edmund he
actually enjoyed the touch of scandal. And I swear there was
never any suggestion of..."

"I believe it," I said.

"He taught me everything. How to dress, the easy manner,

the right people to snub and the right people to flatter and where and what and all that dreary fashionable talk. Soon people began automatically to ask me wherever he went. In a way I was sort of a project with him."

"You mean he was playing Svengali to your Trilby."

"If you like. Anyway, he seemed to be a sort of magician who could open Pandora's box. We dined and spent weekends with people who had been only names on the front pages of newspapers to me. Prime Ministers. Kings and ex-Kings. Everyone seemed to treat him with such respect. I never for a minute doubted that he was above reproach. We would be in Berlin one week and dining with Chamberlain in London the following and all the time he spoke of 'avoiding war at all costs!' "

"You know from which end of the horse that came."

"I didn't know then."

She stopped a moment to light a cigarette, then continued: "In London I met Reggie Fayne. He was in the Foreign Office at the time. He and Edmund seemed to have become great friends and Edmund was enthusiastic about Reggie's 'great future.' He kept talking about his 'plans' for Reggie. When Reggie fell in love with me, he seemed delighted. It would make what he termed 'a good match.' Reggie's family is one of the oldest in England. The wedding was one of the most fashionable of the season despite the family's coolness. Edmund gave me away—which delighted the gossips."

She began her pacing again. "It was right after the wedding that the trouble started. Edmund had invited us to spend our honeymoon on his yacht off Monte Carlo and it had been more or less understood that we would accept. But suddenly Reggie said 'no' and we went to Antibes instead. Reggie refused to discuss his reasons for refusing Edmund's invitation. At the time I put it down to jealously and I was rather annoyed with what I considered pettiness. After that we didn't see Edmund again. Reggie would get furious every

time I mentioned his name. After the war broke out Reggie
and I lived in Paris for a while where he was, I thought, on
some mission for his government. And then, after the inva-
sion, we were in Vichy. One day he discovered that I was se-
cretly corresponding with Edmund who was in Spain at the
time. He was furious, and this seemed to me, at the time,
unforgivable. He accused him of collaboration with the
Nazis, among other things. It seemed childishly stupid. I
simply couldn't believe that Edmund, whom I considered
so wise and kind, was in league the Nazis. It developed into
a violent argument. The servants must have overheard. I
lost my head and told him about Edmund's veiled implications in his letters. That it was actually Reggie who might
be a Nazi agent. And that I must persuade Reggie to come
to Spain where he, Edmund, would give Reggie another
chance for my sake. Reggie went white to the lips. I'll never
forget the look in his eyes. He turned on his heel and left the
room. That night he was turned over to the police as a Nazi
collaborator. Grayle came to me the next day..."

"Grayle! He was in Vichy?"

"Yes. He had been there about a week."

"Go on," I said. I managed to keep the excitement out of
my voice.

"He told me I must take Charles and escape from France
before I too was implicated in Reggie's crime. It never occurred to me that Edmund was not sure of his facts. Even
though I was so fond of Reggie I was still very much under
the spell of Edmund's personality. I wouldn't have believed
it if anyone had told me it was Edmund who was working
with the enemy. We fled to the Spanish border. I didn't hear
of Reggie's death until three weeks later. After I had already
joined Edmund in Lisbon. After that nothing seemed to
matter much. I had been fond of Reggie. I don't believe I
was really in love with him. But Edmund convinced me that
my husband was a Nazi collaborator."

"Do you still believe it?"

"No," she said, flatly.

"And Edmund?"

"I haven't decided yet. All I know is I want to take Charles away from here. I want to go home to the States."

I took time to light a cigarette. She made it almost sound convincing. I couldn't understand her motive for clearing out but felt there must be some hidden reason. Perhaps a rich lover in New York or the feeling that Marlan's well had been pumped dry.

"You make yourself out pretty naïve," I said.

"Maybe I do. Perhaps there is one thing I haven't made clear enough. The attraction Edmund had for me. Up to then there was a price tag on everything I wanted in life. I seemed to have spent my early years fighting off men. My own father was bitter and surly. We were never close. Marlan was the first person ever to be kind to me. I would have done anything for him. Yes, whatever he asked. I felt that beneath his sophistry and bitter wit he was a great human being. It was all fantasy, I know now, but his hold over me was magnetic."

"You've gone to a helluva lot of trouble to tell me all this..."

She crossed the room and stood over me, very tense and serious.

"I have a reason, Gil."

"What's that?"

"I don't trust anyone any more. I suppose I have less reason to trust you than any of them. But I do. If anything should happen to me, I want you to promise to take Charles back to the States."

I reached for her. It's an atavistic notion. You don't think about it until after you do it. I reached for her and I forgot my suspicions and my conclusions and my conscience and I pulled her against me so that my body understood her in braille. If I had a conscious thought it was that she responded almost immediately, a thing which does not often happen in women. She responded like a girl running for her life—fast, furiously, half-crying and without regard to feminine dignity.

Once she said "Gil!" as though some swift unexpected pain caused her to exchange consciousness for the sensory anesthesia she preferred. But it was only for the moment and soon her eyes were heavy-lidded and the intense expression on her face added some years to Claire as I knew her.

It was a cheap trick on my part. Claire had been alone and unloved for a long time and there was shameless hunger for the close smell of a man. I had sensed it and I had held food too close to the starving. Now I knew that I had done it on purpose; subconsciously maybe, but it had been done with malice aforethought.

Afterward, she stared at me from the bed, her hands lifeless at her side. I fixed my tie and combed my hair with my hands. I could see her behind me through the vanity mirror. She sat up and stretched and arched her back like a cat who has eaten fully and would now like to doze before the ruddy flicker of a fireplace.

"Claire," I said, without turning. The stretch continued. I put my coat on and walked out.

Chapter 14

It took twenty-four hours to track down Pinel. For a time I thought Ali had betrayed me but finally at eleven o'clock the following night he knocked on my door and told me that Pinel was waiting in a small pension near the Mecca gate. I went native again in fez and burnoose and left the house by the way of the servants' entrance with Ali at my side. The guards didn't even give us a second glance as we slipped out through the service gate.

The Italian pension was called Il Capri and it was an incredibly filthy hole even by Near Eastern standards. I found Pinel waiting for me in a large room containing an enormous bed, and one broken chair. The bed was covered with torn mosquito netting, the floor was stone, the plastered walls were cracked.

Pinel was lying on the bed. He propped himself up on one elbow as I came in.

"You have nerve," he said dryly. "That I will credit you."

"Thanks," I said, "I've come to make a report."

He didn't ask me to sit. Instead he regarded me through half-closed eyes and said, "This should prove interesting."

"It is," I said. "If you can arrange to charter a plane I will see to it that Claire Fayne leaves for Algiers. As soon as possible."

Slowly he swung his legs over the edge of the bed. His expression was set. "You went to the office of Sirauc after you left the Chez Lautrec, against my orders. You went there and after you left Gaby Duval was found dead."

"Now listen, Pinel, I..."

His hand snapped up in a gesture of command. "No. Wait. The next day I find you lunching at Edmund Marlan's. You will tell me no doubt that it was in the line of duty. And perhaps that is the truth. Where are you living now?"

"At Mrs. Fayne's house. Marlan is out for my skin."

"And that also could be the truth."

There was a moment's silence.

"I for one do not believe that you killed Gaby. I cannot believe that you are in Marlan's pay. However, I might as well tell you, Gil, that I am almost alone in this belief. You are an admitted mercenary. A man without honor."

I felt the blood rising to my face. "It's different now. I'm not doing this for the cash. Not since they killed Gaby."

"What is this about chartering a plane?"

I told him of Claire Fayne's expressed wish to make a get-away. He looked thoughtful.

"It is a hard one to swallow," he said after a moment. His voice was tired. He stood up and began pacing back and forth. After a bit he stopped in front of me. "If this is a double-cross, so help me, Gil, it is the last double-cross you will ever pull. I am willing to give you a chance. I remember things the others know nothing of. I remember you before. But if you are, how you say, playing ball with Mrs. Fayne or Marlan I will kill you with my own hands."

"I wouldn't blame you," I admitted. And I felt a sudden uneasiness. Could I be sure that Claire Fayne would really go through with the plan? Looking up into Pinel's face, I knew that if she balked at the last minute it would mean my death warrant.

"You understand?" he said.

"Completely!"

He turned his back on me, took a pad and pencil from an inner pocket and sat once more on the bed. His manner was brusque and businesslike.

"Now then, tell me how and why Mrs. Fayne has decided to walk so docilely into our hands."

I explained everything that had happened. Halfway through my recital I noticed that he had stopped taking notes and once more the doubt was back on his face.

"Can you arrange about the plane?" I asked.

"Yes."

"How soon?"

He thought for a moment. "Today is Tuesday. All arrangements will have been completed before the end of the week." He shoved the pad back into his pocket. "I will let you know before Thursday a.m. It is better for you to remain at Mrs. Fayne's until I can give you final instructions. In the meantime you can tell her the arrangements are being made but there must be no atmosphere of imminent departure in her house. When the time comes she must be ready to leave quickly. No more luggage than two small bags."

"All right."

I stood. Pinel was watching me sharply. He didn't move. After a moment, he said, "What's wrong?"

"Wrong? I don't get it."

"What are you doubtful about, Denby?"

"It's not my job to doubt," I said with a shrug. I took a step to the door, turned and blurted out, "Listen, Pinel. There's just a chance, a bare chance that her story is on the level. What then?"

"Ah?" He got to his feet. "She must be good in bed," he said harshly.

I controlled my anger. "Don't be a goddamned fool. I'm delivering the dame to you. All I said was, suppose..."

"She will have a trial."

"We know the circumstantial evidence is against her. There aren't many people to testify to her innocence if she is innocent. You know damned well that the minute she lands in Algiers, she's a dead duck."

"Since when have you returned to being the great defender of justice, Denby?"

"Never mind that. If I am convinced she was responsible for Gaby's death your chartered plane won't be necessary. I'll save you the expense of a trial. That's how I feel. All I'm asking is, if..."

"I wouldn't waste time on academic questions, Denby. Get back to your job and let us not worry about the ethics involved."

I shrugged with more indifference than I felt.

"Stay undercover until you hear from us," he said.

"O.K." When my hand was on the doorknob he said, "It is better to speak plain. Remember, if this is a double-cross, you will never leave Teheran alive."

There wasn't anything more to be said. I went out into the

murky hallway. Ali was waiting for me in the small lobby.
When we were in the street he offered me a cigarette. As I
took it from the package he said, "Your hand is shaking."

"I once had malaria," I said. "It comes back now and
again."

"Yes," he said, "I see."

Chapter 15

Claire entertained Marlan and some of his stooges at dinner
that night. Ali brought my dinner in on a tray.

"Tell me, Ali," I asked him. "Just what is it you people
want?"

" 'You people,' sir?"

I indicated the Persian Cat. He looked from the cat to my
face impassively. After a moment he said, "It is not good to
be poor anywhere in the world, sir. But it is worse to be poor
and also a Moslem."

"So you are turning to the north. Do you think you will
find freedom from that quarter?"

"You are mistaken, sir," he said quietly. "We want no outside help. All we ask is freedom to work out our own des-
tiny."

"Freedom from whom?"

"It is the same all through the Moslem world. The poor
stay poor. The western world heeds us not. They hear only
the words of the muftis and the shahs and the effendis, the
men who are made rich by selling our labor and cooperating
with the rich of other countries."

"The Arab League?"

He smiled bitterly. "A rich man's scheme," he said. "Some
great powers encourage it for their benefit. In return they
get oil. It is time all this ends. Some day it will end."

"Where does a man like Marlan stand in your plans?"

His expression became guarded. "Is there anything else you wish, sir?"

"No thank you, Ali."

Later that evening when Claire came to my room she seemed nervous and worried. "Did you make the arrangements?" she asked.

"We'll know the details by Thursday."

"How soon will it be?"

"Before the end of the week."

She was pacing back and forth. "I wish it were tonight, Gil. I'm frightened."

"Was something said at dinner to frighten you?"

"It's what was not said. Your name wasn't even mentioned. Edmond looks like a cat who has swallowed the mouse. Don't you see, Gil. He doesn't seem at all disturbed by your escape. On the contrary I got the impression several times that he *knew*."

"Don't get imaginative," I said. "There's no possible way for his knowing I'm here. Not unless Ali is an informer, which I don't believe. Or..." I stopped.

"Or what?"

"Or you have told him."

She stopped pacing and turned angrily on me. "Don't be a damned fool."

"I was kidding," I said lightly. She relaxed and sat in the small chair near the window. Outside, behind her head, a rigid moon was pasted on the night sky.

"Gil," her voice was deadly serious. "You promised, if anything should happen to me, that you would see Charles safely out of this."

"Nothing is going to happen to you." I wasn't looking at her as I said it.

"But suppose it does. I've been thinking. I wanted Charles to be brought up in the States. But I have no one there. No relations who could take him. I'm afraid there's only one solution."

"What's that?"

"Reggie's family in England. I believe they would take him, if I were out of the picture."

I didn't answer. I was thinking of Charles, who dreamed of baseball and a red brick schoolhouse near some street called Main, lost in the stuffy depths of an English country house and growing to lonely maturity amid the crumbling relics of a dying life. It wasn't what he wanted, but it seemed the only choice. And I thought of the staid British family and how they would face the news that their grandson's mother had died as a traitor before a firing squad.

Claire refused to stay with me that night. Her mind seemed far away on other things. Uneasily I wondered whether she had some premonition of the truth. After she had left me I found sleep impossible. Dawn was creeping over the distant minarets before I finally dozed off. The following morning Ali delivered to me a note from Pinel. "Arrangements set for tonight. Our car will stop for you, Mrs. Fayne, and the boy at nine p. m. by the servants' entrance. Chartered plane will take off from the estate of M. Treier five miles north of Teheran at nine-fifty-five. See that there are no slip-ups. Pinel."

When I told Claire, she seemed startled. "But Gil. I thought arrangements would be made by Friday at the earliest."

"Last night you wanted to go immediately."

She avoided my eyes. "There are some things I must..."

"Like what?"

For a moment she didn't answer. I noticed that the chiffon handkerchief she carried had been squeezed into a ball. After a while she said, "You're quite right, of course. The sooner the better."

She didn't come near me again until late afternoon. The day seemed to drag on interminably. As evening approached

I felt a growing tension in the air. I was convinced that Claire planned no trap, that she was sincere in her desire to get away from Marlan, yet I couldn't throw off the feeling that somewhere, something had gone wrong. I thought I'd never heard the house so silent. It was a stifling hot day and the sky was blinding white.

She came in about five followed by Ali who carried a tray holding the cocktail mixings and glasses.

"You are to stay here, sir," Ali said. "I will knock at your door at quarter of nine. You will join Mrs. Fayne and the boy at the servants' entrance as soon as possible."

"Roger."

When he left I fixed the cocktail and handed one to Claire. She looked at it ruefully.

"Thank God for martinis," she said. "They've helped me get through some of the tougher spots."

"Maybe some day there will be a race of men who drink them for divertissement rather than through necessity."

"Maybe." She attacked the drink in a business-like manner. I chattered a little but she seemed thoughtful and preoccupied. After a bit I stopped the chatter and asked, "What's wrong, Claire?"

"I'm a little sad."

"Why?"

"Oh, I don't know. Thinking about how things might have been, for instance."

"In what way?"

Instead of answering, she asked me, "Gil, tell me what you were like before. Before you became a soldier."

"Sexual habits? Politics? Financial status?"

"Anything, as long as you don't make a joke of it."

I poured another drink to gain time. All that "before" business. I'd almost forgotten.

"I went to school in Houston, college in Texas..."

"What is your family like?"

"*Was*, you mean. My mother died when I was twelve. My old man was a real estate broker with a nice sum in the bank, a bright new house in the right part of town, membership in a few of the right clubs. During my early teens I played golf and danced and laid a few of the right debutantes. My old man was the kind of a guy you might have met that day at the country club when you met Marlan. I was just an ordinary American dope until about my second year in college."

"What happened then?"

"Darned if I know exactly. I began reading things. Thinking about things. I noticed new things, too. The way Jews never made a good fraternity and the way the Negroes lived. I got to be one of those sophomoric liberals. Insufferable really. A first class intellectual snob."

"I bet you were nothing of the kind."

"When stuff began happening in Spain I wanted to go. But my old man developed a heart condition and I had to leave college to run his business and got a job on a newspaper in Houston. After a year I went to Detroit for a paper there. I was in Detroit when war broke out and I joined up with all the fervor of a Latter-day Saint. It took a long time for the halo to wear thin."

"There must have been a girl somewhere along the line."

"There were plenty of them."

"No one in particular?"

Before I knew it I was telling her about Dorothy. About the way we used to sit around in dives until dawn listening to swing music and talking Hemingway dialogue. And how it got so I couldn't think of anything else. And her promises. "She was a lot like so many who promised to wait. But she was ambitious. A year after I went overseas she was married to some rich bastard with a couple million. I never heard from her again."

She said nothing for a moment. Then, very quietly, very seriously, she said, "I wish I had known you the second year at college, Gil. I wish I had known you before I met Marlan."

"What the hell," I said. "Neither of us was made for a little white house on Main Street. We would have driven each other nuts."

"No," she said. "No, we wouldn't. It's what you want now, really. I know that. And it's what I want but it's too late for me."

I looked at her, sitting there like something out of last month's *Vogue*, chic and lovely, an expensive fixture for a millionaire's yacht and I laughed. She didn't flinch nor did she seem annoyed. She simply accepted it.

"Anyway," she said. "I want you to know, Gil, I'm very grateful for having known you."

She stood as though suddenly weary, as though the effort of getting to the door were too much. "There's something I want you to know about yourself." She went on slowly, "Something I know better than you do."

"What's that?"

"No matter how much you may kid yourself into believing you're a hardboiled mercenary, you'll never do anything really evil. You're not made like Marlan. You belong on the other side, Gil. Always."

A feeling of shame and anger overcame me. I began, "For Christ's sake..."

She smiled. "Just remember that. You're the kind of a man I'd like Charles to be." She was at the door.

"Claire!" I had a sudden mad desire to tell her everything. To tell her of the way she had been tricked and of the trap into which she was walking. But she lifted her hand and said, "Shh, darling. Tell me later."

The door closed behind her. I poured the remainder of the shaker into my glass and gulped it down. It was a trick, of course. The sort of a trick she had played on Reggie and Marlan and God knows how many men. And yet I had to use all the willpower at my command to keep from following her, to keep from warning her, to throw the whole thing over and maybe try to make a getaway with her. But even if I had been so foolish as to obey the impulse I knew there was no place to run to any more. This was the dead end. There was only one opening in the wall and Pinel was holding that door.

It's a stinking, crazy world, I thought. I love her. I love her more than I loved Dorothy or any of the others. But not enough for that.

With the empty glass I wandered to the window. I felt sick and depleted. The day was fading fast. The sunbaked city was suffused in an unnatural yellowish light. Down below me a native was making his way across the lawn. He seemed to glide along like a shadow in a dream, like a shadow without purpose or destination.

Chapter 16

I looked for the hundredth time at my watch: eight-forty-five. Ali had not been in with my dinner. Without actually hearing any sound I had the sensation of activity in the house around me. I imagined men whispering and soft padded feet creeping down the halls. Outside the window I could see small black clouds scudding swiftly across the stars and the face of the moon. I went to the door, placed my ear against the panel and listened. There was nothing. No sound. Nothing.

It was queer, I thought, Ali's not coming with a dinner tray. He'd always been punctual. And yet, I told myself, nothing has gone wrong. Nothing can happen to spoil the plan now. Everything's going to be all right.

As I stood listening at the door I thought I heard a faint sound like the snapping of a twig. I froze there, tense and waiting. Then I put my hand in my pocket and released the safety on the revolver Ali had given me that morning.

A minute passed. The sound was not repeated. A faint breeze had sprung up in the night and behind me the curtains at the window fluttered. The feeling of uneasiness increased.

Clouds in the sky were almost unheard of this time of year. A breeze was unnatural. The atmosphere seemed charged with electricity. Even the room to which I had become accustomed had an odd look.

Outside in the hall, there was a faint rustling sound. Before I had a chance to straighten up there was a soft knock on the door. Quickly I stepped back, one hand on the revolver and said, "Who is it?"

"Ali."

I unlocked the door.

"Come," Ali whispered. "It is time."

I followed him out into the dimly lit corridor. Ahead of us light spread up from the main stairwell, but Ali turned in the opposite direction from the light and with a finger to his lips in caution, led the way towards the rear of the house. As directed I was dressed in the burnoose and my clumsy movements sounded to me like the flapping of bat's wings.

We went around a corner and down another long corridor and then through a door which led out into the landing of a narrow flight of stairs, which I assumed were ordinarily used by the servants. At the top we hesitated a moment, listening. Then we started swiftly down. Just as we reached the second floor, a door swung open and a native servant gave us a startled look. I drew back, but almost immediately the servant's face went blank and he backed up, allowing the door to close between us.

Arriving at the bottom, I followed Ali into an empty pantry, through a deserted kitchen, out into a small garden. There beside the door, stood another servant and by his side, dressed in Arab style, Charles. The boy's eyes shone with excitement.

"Where is Mrs. Fayne?" I asked Ali.

He exchanged a few words with the servant, then turned to me, his face impassive. "Hajid say Mrs. Fayne says to go ahead. She will meet you at the estate of M. Trelier."

The feeling of shock crystallized into anger.

"Oh, she does, does she! Where is she?"

"We have not time," Ali said hastily. "You must go on with the boy now. The car is outside the wall waiting."

"Look, Ali. Don't argue. Take the boy to the car. Tell M. Pinel to wait another few minutes. Where is Mrs. Fayne?"

"In her room," he said quietly.

"Go ahead with the boy."

"That's right," Charles whispered. "You make her come now, Gil."

Ali seemed about to remonstrate, apparently changed his mind, shrugged and started down the garden path towards the servants entrance. I went quickly back into the strangely deserted kitchen and through the pantry and dining room into the front part of the house. No one was in sight, a fact which in itself was disturbing in this house of many servants.

When I got to the second floor I went into Claire's room without knocking. She was standing looking from the window and when I came in, she turned. She wore a black dinner dress with sapphires glittering at her throat. I'd never seen her look more beautiful, pale and still, her face remote, showing only slight surprise.

"Is that how you dress for traveling!" I said.

"Don't be a fool, Gil. Edmund telephoned. He wanted to stop in. I couldn't put him off. He would have been suspicious if he had found me gone. You must take Charles to the airplane and wait until I can safely get away."

I took a step towards her. "You're lying."

She shrugged.

"Claire, for Christ's sake, you'd let Charles go like that, alone?"

She turned away, but not soon enough to hide the sudden pain in her eyes.

"Please go, Gil."

"I'm not leaving here without you!"

"You can't be that stupid. Marlan will be suspicious if I'm not here when he arrives. We'd never get away. I'll join you at M. Trelier's place. Ali will take me in my own car."

"You know damned well you have no intention of joining us at the airport!"

I strode across the room and grasped her by the shoulders. She looked about her like a trapped animal.

"What the hell are you up to?" I said savagely.

She didn't answer. She avoided my eyes. As my hands tightened on her shoulders, she gave no sign of pain. She seemed almost indifferent.

And then suddenly I heard the sound of a car coming up the drive. She came to life. There was real panic in her eyes. She looked wildly about the room as though searching for something.

"All right," she said suddenly. "I'll come with you."

I relaxed my hold. She grabbed up a wrap and a bag from the chaise-longue and started to fumble with the catch on the bag.

"What the hell..." I began.

"My passport," she explained breathlessly. "I've got to be sure."

The car sounded as though it were almost at the entrance. Her hand came out of the bag holding a revolver.

"Now get out!" she said. "Quick!"

Downstairs a car door slammed. I knew suddenly it was no use.

"You bitch!" I said.

Her face was tight and her eyes had a wild lost look in

them.

"Goodbye, Gil," she said. "Goodbye, darling."

Very faintly I heard voices in the lower part of the house. I turned and left the room. There was no time to lose, no time to think, no time to regret. I found the service stairs and hurried down, through the pantry and kitchen, out into the garden. Back there all was quiet. I found the archway and went out into the alley where the car was drawn up close to the wall, its lights blacked out.

The rear door opened and I jumped in. Pinel said, "Where is she?"

"Tell them to drive on," I said. "There's been a slip-up. Marlan is in the house. She'll join us as soon as she gets rid of him." I didn't believe it, of course, I was simply stalling for time.

Charles was in the rear of the car with Pinel and myself. At the wheel was an Arab chauffeur and beside him, Lautrec.

"Slip-up!" Pinel's voice was harsh with fury.

"You go on to the plane with the boy," I said. "Yes. That's it. Better that way. I'll wait for her." I started to reach for the door, but Pinel shoved me back roughly.

"So!" he said. "They were right after all!"

"No one could foresee Marlan would appear at this time." But my voice was listless.

"Tell your man to drive on," Pinel said sharply to Lautrec. "This place is a trap!"

Lautrec muttered something to the driver and the car's motor sprang to life. We began to move slowly down the alley.

Pinel said, "We have the boy. Maybe that will bring her to her senses. We'll have to figure out what we're going to do about you."

We hit the main highway to the city. Pinel suddenly leaned forward and said sharply, "He's going the wrong way, Lautrec. We go back to the city and right through it to the north gate."

"I'm afraid not," said Lautrec. He had twisted around until he was facing us. He had a revolver. Pinel slowly sank back in the seat.

"So! You're all in it together. Does everyone in the world work for Marlan?"

"Everyone with any brains," Lautrec said.

"Me then, I've got no brains," I said.

Pinel gave me a quick look. "You can come out in the open now, Denby. You've got me where you want me."

"I'm still working for you," I said. "And I have been all along."

Pinel said nothing. The car was speeding out towards the open country. Lautrec's ruined face watched us. After a moment Pinel said wearily, "And you a Frenchman, Lautrec."

Lautrec sneered. "What difference does the nationality make any more? It is not good to have a flag and no money in the pocket. I'm swimming with the tide like any sane fish."

Ahead of us a car was drawn up beside the road. We began to slow down. I saw that the car was the black Rolls in which I had been transported from the Provençal to Marlan's house. We came to a stop. Drexel stepped out of the Rolls, followed by two natives. And from around the front of the car came Haussan, Marlan's sadistic chauffeur.

"Good evening," Drexel said pleasantly. "You will all come with me in the Rolls. It is so much more comfortable."

"What sort of entertainment do you have in mind for us?"

Drexel shrugged delicately. "That, of course, is up to Mr. Marlan."

"How did you find out?" Pinel demanded.

Drexel indicated Lautrec with a polite gesture. The Frenchman averted his eyes. "We have known from the moment Denby hid himself in Mrs. Fayne's house," he said.

"Did *she* tell Marlan?"

"Come," Drexel said. "We must not waste time."

We started to get out of the car. Charles had said not a word. His face was pale, but he obeyed without question. As we stepped down into the sandy road, I saw far away towards town the lights of a car. They seemed to be coming very fast.

Drexel noticed them at the same time.

"What's that?" he said sharply.

"Probably some one headed out towards Grezian," Lautrec said. But I could tell he, too, was uneasy. "Hurry!" he said.

Erect and disdainful, Charles marched ahead towards the Rolls with Pinel at his heels. Slowly, I started across the few yards separating me from the car. I was acutely aware now of the approaching lights. I stumbled and fell to one knee. Something jabbed me viciously in the ribs. I looked up into Haussan's dark face.

"Cut that out!" Drexel hissed at me. "No tricks now."

The headlights of the approaching car danced over the scene. Haussan and Drexel were trying to look as though they were assisting me. We were almost to the running-board of the Rolls.

And then I heard the screeching of brakes.

"Someone's curious," Drexel whispered. "Careful now, Haussan."

The car, a dilapidated old touring car, came screeching to a stop. It was filled to overflowing with natives. It looked not unlike a load of soiled laundry. Haussan wheeled about and I saw the long curved knife in his hand. Drexel had taken out a revolver. Lautrec and the three Arab drivers came running up from the front car. The soiled laundry began to disintegrate, spilling in all directions with amazing rapidity, even before the old touring car had come to a complete halt.

There were no shouts, no curses, no screams. Only heavy breathing, a sob, a groan disturbed the silence of the night.

And the curious, eerie sound of feet padding softly on the dirt road.

In the moonlight, steel blades gleamed. Haussan threw himself into the midst of the soiled laundry. Pinel had thrown himself between Lautrec and Charles. No words were spoken, there was something deadly and utterly final in the struggle beside the moonlit road. In the midst of the soiled laundry I saw Ali's face shining with rage and triumph. A shot rang out and one of the natives fell with a groan. I found myself struggling with Haussan, the Arab driver of Marlan's Rolls. His face was close; I could see the whites of his eyes and smell his foul breath. My feet slipped in the dry dust. I felt myself falling. Someone caught me from behind. I saw the half-mad face of the Arab poised above me and then behind him the gleaming knife and suddenly the face opened, gasped, fell away from me and there stood Ali. I leaped to my feet. Pinel was fighting off Lautrec and the other driver. I saw Ali's men swarm about them. And then I saw Drexel disappearing around the back of the Rolls.

I moved quickly, filled now with deadly purpose. Another shot was fired. Somewhere behind me there was a gurgling sound. I didn't turn, I saw only Drexel moving like a shadow down the road towards town. I followed him, feline in my silent pursuit, my feet making no sound in the thick yellow dust. The moon was on his back. He half turned and his face reflected white in the moonlight. He jumped swiftly to one side, crouched, and there was a small explosion of sound.

The shot went wild; I never stopped. He still crouched there, trusting the revolver and then I saw a frantic, desperate movement of the shoulders. The revolver was either jammed or else he had run out of ammunition. He threw the gun from him, turned uncertainly and then ran off into a field to the right of the road. I followed into the knee-high grass, gaining on him. He began to zig-zag crazily as though afraid that any direction he took was the wrong one. His arms flailed about as though he were incapable of controlling their motion.

Suddenly he fell. Apparently he had tripped over a rock or stumbled in a ditch. He tried to scramble to his feet. I could hear his breathing. He sounded like an exhausted hound. Before I fell on him he began to sob.

I literally hurled myself on him, smashing my fist into his face as I fell. He fought like a half-mad woman, tearing at me with his finger nails, spitting and sobbing, begging for mercy in frantic, disjointed phrases.

"You killed Gaby!" I shouted. I held him flat against the ground and drove my fist once more into his throat. He stopped struggling and lay there, suddenly resigned, with his eyes half closed.

"Who killed Gaby?"

There was no answer. I thought for a moment that he had passed out. But as my fingers began to tighten about his windpipe, he suddenly gasped, "It was Grayle."

"Grayle! How could that delicate little flower kill anyone?"

He seemed to sense my doubt. "You don't know. He likes to kill. He likes it."

I relaxed my grip on his throat. He didn't move any more. Waiting, I brought my fist up like a hammer, thinking of lots of things all at once. Gaby and others. Men I had known who were dead. Then I put my fist down into the middle of his face. There was a crunching sound and then he lay still.

Slowly I got to my feet. The night was deathly still. All sounds of the struggle near the cars had ceased. The moonlight cast a bluish light over the fields. The unconscious man at my feet twitched. Someone was coming across the fields. I turned defensively but when I saw it was Pinel I relaxed. It was not until he was almost beside me I saw the revolver in his hand.

"Come on," he said harshly.

"Where?"

"We're going back to get Mrs. Fayne. That's why we came to Teheran."

I walked in front of him, feeling exhausted and devoid of thought. When we reached the cars I saw Haussan stretched out in the road, his face turned up to the moon. There was a hole above his right eye. He was as stiff as iron. The two Arab drivers were bound up on the side of the road, tied to one another, staring at us with wide, terrified eyes. Charles was in the rear of the Rolls. He was crying. Lautrec stood by the running board trembling. Two of Ali's men stood guard over him with rifles but Ali and the others had disappeared in the black touring car.

"We can thank the Persian Cat," I said.

Pinel opened the front door of the Rolls.

"Get in behind the wheel," he told me.

"Pinel," Lautrec said. His teeth were chattering. "I will explain everything. I was forced to do it. I would never betray..."

"Pig!" Pinel spat out the word. "Take him with you," he said to the natives. "Whatever you do with him is all right with me."

"For the love of God," Lautrec pleaded, "don't leave me with these madmen."

Pinel disregarded him. I got in behind the wheel of the Rolls.

"Gil," Charles whispered from the back. "They killed a man."

"Everything's going to be all right, Charlie," I said with more conviction than I felt. "Don't let it get you down."

He stopped sobbing. "I'm not afraid," he said defiantly.

Pinel got in beside me. Lautrec was screaming hysterically in the road, with a silent, white robed man at either side of him. I started the motor, and began to turn the clumsy car around. I shut my ears to the sound of Lautrec's cries. As we passed him I could hear him shout, "It's not my fault!"

"It never is," Pinel said quietly.

Soon Lautrec and his guards were tiny shadows in the overhead mirror. We raced down the road back towards Mrs. Fayne's house.

Chapter 17

I turned off the motor and the car glided silently down the alley and came to a halt by the wall behind the house.

"What are you going to do?" I asked Pinel.

"Come with me!" He reached for the door handle but I put my hand on his arm and said in an undertone, "The kid..."

"He'll have to stay here alone."

"Alone?"

Pinel shrugged expressively. I turned back to Charles. "Look here, old man," I said. "We need a little cooperation. Someone to stay here and keep an eye on the car."

He looked like a plenty worried kid.

"There'll be no more fighting, Charlie," I said, almost as if I believed it. "You can help best by staying here. If you see any trouble coming press down on the horn."

The kid came around to the front seat. He looked awfully small behind the wheel. Pinel and I went through the archway into the kitchen garden. I had a sick feeling in my stomach. I thought of what Pinel was about: he'd take her along now even if it involved kidnaping. I knew he was right and yet I had this sick feeling. Instead of making for the kitchen door he led the way around the side of the house into the main garden. I looked up at Claire's bedroom, remembering the moment she had walked in from the bath. It was dark. But the drawing-room was lighted and the French windows separating it from the terrace were open. Almost imperceptibly Pinel had dropped back until he was at my side. And then suddenly he was a little behind me and I was aware of the gun.

"Easy now," he whispered.

We were on the terrace and he beckoned me to draw back into the shadow of a large potted palm. Prepared as I was for almost anything, the scene before us, regarded in juxtaposition to what had just occurred out on the deserted road and in relation to the cynical betrayal that made it possible, aroused in me an almost overpowering fury. Claire and Marlan were on the sofa, Grayle nearby. They were all drinking cocktails and at the moment Claire's laughter rang out gay and undisturbed. Grayle, slim and pale in his dinner clothes. Marlan like a figure in a Rembrandt.

Almost unconsciously I took a step towards the nearest window but Pinel grabbed my arm.

"No," he whispered. "Not yet."

Everything was unreasonably quiet. The sounds of the city were sounds out of a distant dream. Only their voices reached us, as clearly as though we had been in the room with them. They were obviously people who were certain of their safety, sure of themselves, amused at the stupidity of their enemies.

"But Edmund," Claire was saying in a chiding tone, "You of all people should know that a woman loathes being underrated."

"Underrated?" Marlan's voice was faintly surprised.

"Darling, of course! You told me yourself you didn't object to a 'Captain of the Guards'."

"Then you don't deny you had him hidden in the house?"

"Of course I don't deny it! It was frightfully amusing and I think it dull of you to spoil my fun!"

Marlan took a sip of his glass, hardly touching it to his lips. He kept watching Claire. You couldn't tell anything from the expression on his face. As I watched Claire, something in me, a voice in my stomach, in my guts, in my heart maybe, began to say "no!"

"Are you trying to tell me, Claire, that you never had any intention of running off with this stupid hoodlum?"

Claire's bright laugh was instantaneous. "Edmund! Do I look as though I had dressed for a romantic elopement with a penniless nobody?"

"You would have me believe that he was nothing more or less to you than a momentary diversion?"

"Momentary in the most definite sense of the word, darling."

Grayle giggled. I was thinking, in a few moments he won't have another giggle left for this life. And I wondered whether or not he had giggled when he killed Gaby.

But, unsuspecting, he giggled again and said, "You must admit, Edmund, that in his crude American way, this Denby was rather attractive."

"That will be all from you," Edmund Marlan said sharply. Grayle subsided in his chair. Marlan turned back to Claire. His voice purred. "Now my dear, I want you to listen to me. I know very well that that foolish young man was hiding out in your house. I let the affair alone because I was curious to see how much you had really learned from me. I admit I was pleasantly surprised to find you here tonight instead of trying to make your way to the nearest border with that Texas Romeo. But, to be frank, I am not altogether satisfied with your lighthearted explanation."

Claire got to her feet, poured the cocktail remaining in the shaker into her glass and went to the glass fireplace where she turned to face the two men. Her head was half tilted back; she looked hard and cynical. And yet for the first time I sensed something else beneath the brilliant enamel of her expression. A sort of cold desperation.

"Now, Edmund," she said, "I find it almost grotesque to be in the role of instructor to you. But there are some things

I want you to understand. About me. It's what I meant a few minutes ago when I said you have made the mistake of underrating me."

"Mistake?" For the first time there was some genuine feeling in Marlan's voice, an almost childish, petulant annoyance. Obviously he was not a man to admit mistakes.

"Yes." Claire's voice was cool. "You made the mistake of considering me a simpering ingénue who must be told idiotic fairy tales in order to be kept happy. Or should I say, to be kept 'functioning'?"

"How do you mean?"

"I mean, that like you, I simply have no use for softness. Watery eyed idealists, or juvenile types who go about with pocket sized panaceas for the masses bore the hell out of me. I respect a man who gets what he wants. No matter what it may be, Edmund. Darling, you must realize I have had tremendous respect for you from the beginning."

She was smiling. Cigarette smoke floated slowly upwards in the heavy air. Grayle was obviously amused. But I couldn't tell about Marlan. He was no longer watching Claire.

"You see, Edmund, I've known everything. All along I've known everything. Oh, not all the details, of course. But the general direction and the goal. And I've admired you for it."

Marlan's voice cracked out like dry wood splitting. "What do you mean, Claire? Specifically."

She hesitated a moment, as though for a second wind, then said, "Well, for example. That romantic young man, Denby. You don't imagine that I was so stupid as not to realize that he had been connected in some way with the French girl who died so abruptly in the Rue Revjed."

Marlan moved slightly on the sofa. He reached forward but at the last moment the gold glass seemed to repel him and the small hand crept back to his body. Claire continued as though the matters she was discussing were of only passing importance.

"Of course I knew. But Edmund, I was annoyed at the manner in which you tried to deceive me. After all, darling, you cannot imagine that this girl mattered at all to me. Her death was merely an item in the newspapers. I'm sure that, in some way, she proved to be inconvenient to you. That's enough for me. You should have trusted me."

Pinel's fingers were digging into my arm. He prevented me from leaping forward. I watched her white throat, thinking, in a minute...

But the minute passed. And its passing found Marlan with a smile on his face. A small smile, the mere caricature of a smile.

"Claire," he said dryly, "I really do believe that at last you are growing up."

She shook her head impatiently. "But I've been grown up for a long time. You should have known. Tell me, did you kill her yourself?"

Marlan leaned back on the couch. After a considered moment he said, "I don't see that you should be involved in business details, my dear. But if not knowing disturbs you..." He shrugged. Then nodded in the direction of Grayle.

Claire turned to Grayle. "You? I can't believe? Really?"

Grayle looked uncertain, then smirked. Smirked shyly, as though he had just been complimented on a good game of bridge. "It's strange," he said, "all the time, as a child, I used to practically faint at the sight of blood. But Mr. Marlan taught me about my hidden resentments. He made me see things differently. He freed me." His eyes glittered. "I guess it was some sort of a sublimated desire that..."

"Quiet!" Marlan's voice bit him off. "I can't stand this talk of blood or sudden death."

Claire paid no attention to Marlan. Her eyes were fixed on Grayle. Her chin was tilted up and the smile still hovered about her lips. "Did you kill the French girl the same way you killed Reggie?" She spoke quietly. "You killed her because she had a rendezvous with Denby. You meant to get him. And when he didn't show up you had to kill her."

In the stunned silence she turned back calmly to Marlan. "Really," she said. "It was stupid of you, Edmund, to go to so much trouble to put Reggie in what you imagined was 'an ugly light' for my benefit. You know very well that Reggie was never a collaborator. That all the time he was, in his dull, plodding way, working for the British."

Marlan got slowly to his feet. His back was to me so I missed the expression on his face. But Grayle was looking up at Claire in open admiration.

"You see, Edmund," she went on, "that's what I mean by underrating me. I think actually you engineered the whole business in a masterful manner. Mr. Grayle was really the one who turned Reggie and those dreary Frenchmen over to Vichy and the Nazis at your orders. Am I not correct in that assumption?"

"Isn't she marvelous, Mr. Marlan?" Grayle said.

"Quiet!" Marlan began moving towards Claire. There was a tension in his movements I didn't like. But Grayle missed the mood of his employer. "But really, it's so clever of her," he gushed on.

The smile was gone from Claire's face. She stood there before the fireplace, pale and still as a statue. Grayle looked from Marlan to Claire and the brightness died from his face.

"So," Claire said quietly, "you betrayed Reggie to the Nazis and you had the French girl murdered. How many more? How many more, Edmund?"

"You've said enough, Claire," Marlan said coolly. He was quite near her now. "But you must realize, my dear, that simply because you know these things, your position is in no way altered. I expect you to go on as before. You are tied to me, you know."

"Aside from the pleasure derived from turning out a finished product, what is it you really want of me, Edmund?"

"Charles."

Her cocktail glass slipped from her hand was shattered on the hearth. "Charles?" She didn't try to conceal her shock.

"You see, Claire dear, I was very fond of Reggie in the beginning. I thought he was intelligent enough to see that he could find a place for himself in my organization, in our lives. That's why I approved of the marriage. It was only when he refused to spend your honeymoon on my yacht that I got the first inkling of his true character. And as things developed I realized he was utterly hopeless. But in Charles I see the son I never had. I have great plans for him. He won't grow into another Reggie or Denby. He won't become another damned fool."

"What is it you wish him to be," she managed to say, "another... Grayle?"

"No," he said. "Another Edmund Marlan."

After a moment she said, "Yes, I see. Would one of you gentlemen be kind enough to give me a cigarette?"

Marlan took a gold cigarette case from a breast pocket and began to move towards her. Claire started fussing with the catch on her handbag. A chill began to crawl up my spine. Pinel's hand, still holding my arm, was trembling.

Marlan was only about two yards from her when the gun came out of her handbag. He stopped dead. Grayle began to get up.

"Stay exactly where you are. Both of you." Her voice was low pitched now, but steady. Marlan's hand, holding the outstretched cigarette case, was frozen before him.

"Grayle," he said quietly, "do something."

Grayle sank back in his chair. His face became deadly pale.

"This is one time, Edmund," Claire said, "when all your money and power isn't going to do you the slightest bit of good."

"Don't be a fool, Claire. If that gun should accidentally go off and kill me, you'll be executed for it."

"It's worth it," she said. "This is the way I planned it. It won't nearly make up for the mistakes I've made."

"That stupid American, Denby. You love him. He did this to you."

"I love him," she said tonelessly.

Pinnel's grip on my arm had relaxed but I found myself unable to move forward.

"He helped me to see things clearly," she continued. "Things I have been only vaguely suspecting for a long time. But I knew from the very first night I met him here in this house that he must be working with some group that meant to avenge Reggie's death. I let him believe I thought he was a cynical mercenary. But I knew better. It's not money that interests a man like Denby."

I felt the blood rising to my face. Behind me there was the vague echo of a chuckle.

"But after all," Claire went on. "*This* job is mine to do. Don't move, Edmund."

He took a step backwards. I saw Grayle's hands tightening on the arms of his chair as though he were preparing to spring. Marlan froze again.

"It never occurred to you, Edmund," Claire said, "that there are people in this world who are not for sale. There are plenty of them. Even today. Unfortunately, for a long time I didn't belong to them. People like me encouraged you in your desperate beliefs. I wanted nice things, glamorous places, and, I suppose, power. In a way I'm more responsible than you. In my ignorance."

"Claire!" For the first time there was genuine emotion in Marlan's voice. Fright. "I've done everything for you. I intend to give Charles the best of everything..."

"The best! Murder! Treason! Worse."

"No, listen. You can't be such a fool as to throw away your life for some abstract nonsense. Don't you realize you are merely romanticizing about Denby. He's no better than the rest of us. It's money with him too. And only money. The difference is in stakes: he plays a penny ante game."

"No," she said, "you're wrong. Maybe he's been blinded for a short time. Blinded to what he really is. He talks tough, he pretends it's all for money. But underneath he's as different from you as night and day. People like you have made him think victory over the Nazis might have been in vain. But there are others, lots of them. And he knows it, underneath. And he's on their side. People like that little French girl your henchman murdered!"

Marlan laughed shakily. "You talk like a naïve school girl." Then suddenly he began to speak very fast, desperately, as though now, at last, he fully realized the sands were running out for him. "Listen, Claire, I can forget this evening. I'm willing to forget. We'll go back to New York. You'll have a great position there with me behind you. Charles will have everything."

The explosion came then.

The explosion, a swift movement, a scream. All in one second.

Above the scream, the scream with bubbles in it, the voice shouting half in triumph, half in fear, "Mr. Marlan!"

But it was not Marlan who collapsed on the rug. It was Grayle. In the moment before Claire had squeezed the trigger he had thrown himself in the path of the bullet.

"Mother, mother," he groaned. Marlan backed away from him in distaste. Claire stood there with the gun at her side looking like a sleep-walker who has awakened, teetering on the edge of a high roof.

Grayle's arm stopped twitching. His face relaxed and his head turned like rubber on his neck and was still. I became aware of a clock ticking in the room. I thought, this is just a play and in a moment Grayle will be rising for his curtain calls.

In the silence Marlan said quietly, "That was extremely foolish of you, Claire." He did not seem nervous about the gun in her hand. Apparently he knew Claire could not bring herself to use the weapon again. She looked up almost with indifference as Pinel and I came across the threshold.

Marlan turned and his world evaporated in one swift instant. You could see it on his face. Incredulity followed by crystal clear awareness of the catastrophe he faced. And yet he kept his voice low pitched and calm. "Mrs. Fayne has just had... what the newspapers will call a 'shooting accident,'" he told us.

"That will only be the beginning of the story," I said. I moved to Claire's side and she stood there, half leaning against me, her eyes fixed on the dead man on the rug. Then I felt her body stiffen and she came out of the nightmare.

"Charles! Where is Charles?"

"He's alright, Claire," I said. I was watching Marlan. There was half a smile on his face. His whole expression suggested bored indifference. He was bending over a cigarette box. When I started for him I was checked by Pinel who, gun in hand, stepped between us.

"All of you," he said grimly. "Ahead of me. Out through the French windows. Around through the garden to the car." He spoke in a tense voice, one eye on the hall door.

Marlan shrugged indifferently and stepped aside to let Claire go first. I followed him towards the threshold. Over my shoulder I said to Pinel, "Surely you see where Mrs. Fayne stands now, Pinel?"

"Never mind that now," the Frenchman said.

Instinctively I knew it would happen. I could have prevented it I suppose but somehow I wanted it that way. It happened very suddenly, just as Marlan stepped over the threshold onto the terrace. With a movement so swift and unexpected, especially in a man of his age, he ducked, darted to one side, shoved Claire out of the way, leaped from the terrace and disappeared into the garden.

I started after him.

"Denby," Pinel shouted. "Let him go! There isn't time! The plane!"

"This is mine, Pinel," I called back. "From now on in, this is mine." Had there been time I might have added, "this is mine for Gaby and Claire and little Charles and all the others who have been murdered, trapped or corrupted."

And I wasn't worried now about Pinel's using the gun on me. He knew. He too had been fond of Gaby.

Chapter 18

Nothing moved. The rose bushes, the palms, the statuary and the summer-house were shadows frozen to the moon-swept lawn. I knew he might have a gun although the fact that he had made no gesture towards an inner pocket when Claire had tried to kill him seemed to indicate otherwise. Alert and tense, I crouched low against one of the rose-bushes. I knew the old man was out here somewhere; I felt it the way a hunter sometimes senses the presence of a big cat in the underbrush.

From the other side of the house came the faint sound of footsteps on gravel; probably Claire and Pinel making their way around to the kitchen garden and possible escape. After Grayle's death their minutes were precious. There might not be many more minutes left for any of us. I realized that my one chance had been to make a getaway with Pinel and Claire in the chartered plane before hell broke loose in Teheran; but this was something I had to do. It was not only because of the promise I had made to poor Gaby as she lay twisted and still on the floor of that office, there were other things, many other things. I crouched there waiting to spring.

Behind me the big house was still as a tomb. Apparently

Ali was still out there on the main road with his men, but I wondered what had happened to all the other servants. After a moment I heard the car's motor roar to life and then the crunching of gears and the renewed roar and then gradually the sound dying out to a distant hum in the night. It was a lonely sound; I felt it was the sound of Claire going out of my life forever.

I thought of the things she had said to Marlan before that shot. It was apparent that she had never known the truth about Reggie, that Marlan had convinced her Reggie was a Nazi collaborator. She had never really known anything, poor kid, until too late. I thought again of the things she had said about me and felt the blush rising to my cheeks.

Well, maybe she was right, just a little right anyway. At least, so far, I had never taken money for a lousy cause. And in a way I suppose I had known from the moment I saw Pinel that first night in the cafe that I would take the job. Not for the money but because of some of the things the Frenchman and I had discussed that night in the ditch before we blew up the German troop train.

Too bad that things hadn't turned out differently. I tried not to think of the things that would be "too bad." Like the New England town I would, in all probability, never see. Nor Charles coming home with his first report card, nor Claire standing beneath the fan-light of a doorway on a crisp autumn night and the elm trees black against the naked electric lights. Too bad... too late.

I sensed, rather than saw, the first sign of movement from the opposite end of the garden. Bent low, hugging the bushes, I started for it. The shadow began to move, slithering across the even row of rose-bushes, vaulting the low hedges in a manner not only incredible but eerie in a man of Marlan's age. So unexpectedly swift had been his flight that I was still yards behind him when he reached the far wall.

Then I saw him silhouetted against the top of the wall,

hunched over it, baboon-like, pulling himself over. For a
moment his face was turned back to me, very distinct in the
moonlight, his eyes wide with fright and his complexion the
color of the moon. I made a lunge for his legs, managed for a
second to hold on to one small, twisting foot before he shook
me loose and was gone. Cursing my own ineptness, I leaped
up, grasped the top of the brick wall, pulled myself up and,
in a moment, dropped down on the other side into a narrow
alley. At the far end, in a splotch of yellow light, Marlan was
disappearing around the corner.

I hurried after him, coming out of the alley into one of the
wide residential avenues of the legation quarter. The street
was lined with trees and wide walks like a boulevard in a
quiet section of Paris. Two blocks to the west a horse and
carriage moved lazily down the middle of the avenue; Marlan
was about half way between me and the carriage, cutting
across the avenue on a long angle. There was absolutely no
one else in sight. His footsteps echoed in the silence like the
scamper of mice in panic. In a moment I began to gain on
him. I saw him hesitate a moment, his eyes apparently on
the carriage; then he seemed to change his mind, crossed to
the sidewalk opposite and scurried along, close to the wall. I
wondered where in hell his henchmen were.

He seemed suddenly to be unsure of himself, hugging the
wall, looking back over his shoulder, obviously uncertain as
to whether to continue in a direct line of flight or to dart off
into one of the alleys or gardens on his left. The space between
us began to close.

And then, quite suddenly, I became aware that someone
was following me. Still moving forward I glanced back. No
one was in sight. But the sound was still registering in my
head—the soft patter of feet across asphalt. Just before I
turned front there was the flash of something white from
one of the archways. There wasn't time for more than that
quick glance back. I hoped the burnoose I wore would be

for the moment sufficient disguise.

Who was back there? Surely not Pinel. He and Claire should be almost at the airport by this time. Had someone been hiding in the apparently deserted house as I lay in wait for Marlan? Had there been someone behind a darkened window all the time, watching me?

But I stopped speculating when, up ahead, Marlan suddenly disappeared from view. The robe, whipping about my legs, held me back more than I'd expected, yet even with this handicap I would never have thought that Marlan could have evaded me so easily.

I reached the corner of a narrow street leading off into the maze of alleys behind the Maidan. Marlan was nowhere to be seen. I knew it was futile to pursue him into this labyrinth. For the moment he was safe.

I looked back, down the wide avenue. The street was empty. Perhaps I had imagined that someone was following me. I knew that Marlan would be heading for one place only, the place where his power was the greatest, his palace on the other side of town. I figured he would head for the taxi rank in front of the big European hotel on the square.

In a few minutes I was behind the great mosque, plunging through the heart of the native quarter. If Marlan was able to procure a taxi quickly it would still take him a good five minutes to reach the West Gate by way of the roads open to motor traffic. Although my knowledge of the native quarter was decidedly vague, I knew the way through it was actually a short cut to the West Gate.

The passage in which I found myself was barely four yards wide, a deserted alley full of odd little sounds: a whispered voice behind a black archway, a shutter squeaking shut, a pebble dropping unaccountably on the cobblestones. Somewhere nearby a street festival must have been in progress. I was followed by the dissonant sound of native music and raucous laughter, faint and finally dying away on the night.

The fact that I instinctively chose the right route was more a matter of luck than of navigation; each street and alley looked exactly alike to me and the points of the compass a mere memory. But somehow, and soon, I knew I was in the vicinity of Bagdad Road which left the town through the West Gate.

Up ahead was the sound of traffic and white glare where the alley opened on a main road. Somewhere behind me there was the scuffle of a foot on cobblestones. I wheeled around defensively. The long alley was black; nothing moved and yet I was certain that someone was back there. Tension seemed to grow in the empty alley. I moved in close to the wall, expecting any moment the sound of a shot. But I reached the Bagdad Road safely and ducked quickly around the corner into the protective shadow of an arch. I stayed there for almost two minutes watching the entrance to the alley from which I had emerged, but no one appeared. Despite the refusal of my pursuer to show himself I was beginning to be plenty worried.

I had come out into the wide Bagdad Road almost at the Western Gate, the gate through which Marlan must pass in order to reach his palace. It was possible that he had phoned for his own car from one of the hotels and that by this time he might be surrounded by his henchmen. But I was counting on the fact that most of his men had been engaged in the operation out on the country road from which I had escaped with Ali's help. Through the ancient gate a camel caravan was moving into the city. Some sort of a military official and several gendarmes were making comic opera gestures of rage or despair, or perhaps merely polite greetings to the caravan from where they stood before a small guard house on the opposite side of the road.

The scene had a certain barbaric excitement. Flaring torches, yellow against the night, sent lurid shadows dancing across the sun-baked walls. Rocking camels with glaring eyes and madly swinging necks responded indifferently to the screaming drivers. And from somewhere in the midst of the confusion came the sound of delicately tinkling bells. A ramshackle bus and an old Buick sedan were drawn up to one side of the gate waiting for the caravan to pass in order to leave the city. The Buick interested me most; it was a taxi from the rank at the Majestic Hotel.

Careful not to be spotted by the gendarme on the other side of the road. I crept along the walls until I was nearly opposite the car. My hunch had been right; Marlan was in the rear. He was only a few yards from me, but fortunately he was twisted around in an opposite direction, staring through the back window. His small hands were clutching nervously at his coat. I ducked down and moved in on the car and, crouched below the windows, drew myself up onto the running board, crouched low and held in place by a strong grip on the door handle.

Minutes seemed to pass. I knew I didn't stand a chance if one of the gendarmes should take it into his head to cross to my side of the street, or if I should have the bad luck to be spotted by a casual passerby. But this time things broke my way and finally we began to move slowly forward through the gate. Once we were outside we gathered speed and headed away from the city at a rate that, in my position, was far from comfortable. When we began to slow down for the turn at the gates to Marlan's estate I jumped from the car, took a spill in the ditch without any serious consequences and picked myself up. Apparently I had not been spotted, because the taxi started climbing up the long, sweeping drive towards the main entrance.

There was no sign of Marlan's formidable guards at the gates. Somehow I had expected this, though at the moment I found no logical reason for it. I cut quickly across the lawn towards the marble façade on the hill before me. The palace was in complete darkness. Before I was halfway across the

lawn the taxi which had been standing before the entrance
jolted forward and headed down the drive towards the exit.
As I neared the main house I could see someone standing
on the terrace pounding on the bronze doors.

Carefully I crossed the gravel and concealed myself behind
one of the stone lions at the foot of the steps. It was Marlan
up there frantically banging the great brass knocker. He
cried, "Open up! Haussan! Lars!"

After a moment he turned from the door and his features
were quite distant in the moonlight. He looked terror-
stricken.

Suddenly, as he stood there uncertainly, the bronze doors
slowly swung open and a man carrying a suitcase stepped
out.

"Berkeley!" Marlan's voice was a sob of relief. "What's
happened?"

Berkeley stood there very quietly for a moment, then said
with more than a trace of irony in his voice, "What's happened? Edmund Marlan is dead. Haven't you heard?"

Marlan took a step forward. For a moment his voice re-
gained a little of its former tone of command. "You're drunk."

"A little." Berkeley's voice was insolent. "But what I'm
telling you is true. The news is all over Teheran. Grayle was
murdered by Edmund Marlan and then the old guy committed suicide. Results: the rats have deserted the sunken
ship!"

"What nonsense is this! I saw Grayle murdered myself. It
was Claire Fayne who did it. Something went wrong with
our plans."

"Damned right they went wrong. The Iranian Government
is on your trail for fair. It seems the French have turned over
some very interesting information to them. At any rate the
story of Grayle's murder has been substantiated by Mrs.
Fayne's servants—and the story of your death."

"How could the police believe such a thing? Where is my

body supposed to be?"

"I daresay they will have no trouble producing it when the time comes."

"But Haussan and Lars?"

"One of them is dead. The other is in the custody of the police. The rest are heading out. Cairo, Marseilles, New York. Wherever they can find another Edmund Marlan to employ them. The king is dead, long live the king."

"You'll regret this joke, Berkeley," Marlan shouted in a shaking voice.

"Being out of a job is never a joke!"

"Are you all traitors?" Marlan asked.

Berkeley seemed to consider this for a moment, then said, "The only loyalty we ever had, any of us, was to the sense of security you gave us, Marlan. That's gone now, and there's nothing owed." He started to move towards the top of the steps.

"Help me, Berkeley!" The old man's voice was a croak now. "I'll make it worth your while."

Berkeley laughed "This is one we lost, Marlan. We would have been wiser to have gotten rid of Denby in the beginning. We shouldn't have bungled it that night Grayle waited for him at the French girl's. But as it is, c'est finis. The police are probably headed this way now."

Even as he spoke I became aware of the headlights of a car coming to a stop down on the main road near the entrance gate. The lights were dimmed almost immediately and the two men on the terrace seemed unconscious of their danger. I wondered why, if it were the police, they did not come up the drive.

"Where are you going, Berkeley?" Marlan cried.

"East," Berkeley said rather grimly. "I'll have what's left of the British Empire on my tail after tonight. They don't like agents who sell out."

"Where East?"

"Never mind."

"Listen, Berkeley," Marlan's voice was suddenly desperate, this time with hope, "get me to the airport and I'll take care of you. We can clear out. Be in India tomorrow morning. I have funds in Java. You won't have to worry again for the rest of your life."

Berkeley shook off the old man's restraining hand. "Pipe dream. Your airplane pilot is more than likely one of the Iranian boys, one of those damned Persian Cat people. You'd never get further than the outskirts of town and anyone caught with you would be poison. No thanks."

He took a step down off the porch and then turned. There was sudden venom in his voice. "You're done, Marlan. Finished. Don't you realize that the announcement of your death means as far as they are concerned, you're dead already?"

Marlan shrank back from the Britisher as though, finally, at last, he realized the full implications of his predicament. Berkeley looked curiously like a provincial travelling salesman about to leave with the samples of his wares. There was an incongruous air of cocky corruption in his face, a sense of certainty that somewhere soon he would find another Edmund Marlan to whom to tie himself.

He started down the steps, finished, from his attitude, with the shaking decay of a man on the terrace behind him. But he wasn't actually finished. Not quite. I saw that too late to prevent it. But even had I known, I doubt I would have interfered. In the end it was his former employer who gave him his walking papers in the form of a knife in the back. Not figuratively a knife in the back. Not merely the jaunty symbol of our age. But a real knife, long and narrow and buried to the hilt between the Englishman's shoulder blades.

Berkeley teetered on the steps for a moment, an expression of utter astonishment on his face, then the suitcase went clattering down the steps and in a moment he followed, headfirst, plunging face down in the gravel. The knife kept quivering long after Berkeley was still.

For some reason—perhaps because I wanted Marlan to have the next moment of realization alone—I stayed where I was behind the lion. The old man stood there at the top of the steps on the edge of the wide, moonswept terrace with his empty marble house behind him. He looked down at the man he had just murdered. Then he slowly turned and looked all about him, aware at last of his complete isolation.

Then suddenly, as though a cold hand had touched the back of his neck, he wheeled about, crouched low and sprang away from the sight of his own shadow. He leaned against the rail for support and peered fearfully out into the land he owned. He gave a short, shaky laugh and started down the steps, looked wildly about as though each point of the compass offered only some frightful danger.

I stepped from behind the lion.

He didn't see my face. I'm quite convinced that at first he had not the faintest idea who I was. His reaction was an automatic reflex: fear sent him stumbling out across the lawn, running from side to side like a trapped rabbit, heading ever further up the hill towards the summer house.

Dimly I was worried about the car down near the gate, but if the entire Teheran police force had suddenly started up the drive at that moment they could not have prevented me from what I intended to do. Sure of myself, taking my time, I followed him on his mad flight.

Just before he reached the top of the hill, he stumbled, picked himself up and tottered forward into the pseudo-Greek trappings of his summer house. Here on the edge of the pool where only a few days previously he had entertained Teheran at lunch, he clung to one of the marble pillars, sobbing with fright. When he saw me coming he made one final lunge backwards and stumbled over the edge of the pool into the water.

For a moment I stood there listening to him thrashing about in the water. At first he didn't cry out. The fury began to die within me. I felt tired and empty. Vaguely I was aware of the white runner swan bobbing up and down in the darkness at the other end of the pool.

Finally he managed to cry out, "Can't swim. Help!" And the gasping and the thrashing about.

"Maybe now Gaby can help you," I said. But even as I said it I was stripping off my burnoose. Suddenly I was sick with the violence and the killing. I thought, I'm finished with it. Let the law and his own desperate future take care of him.

I dropped the burnoose on the tiles and stepped to the edge of the pool and was about to dive in when someone grabbed my arm. I ducked and wheeled about to face Ali.

"No," he said quietly. "It is not worth it."

The sounds from the pool had taken on an ominous rhythm. A moment of splashing, a moment of silence, a moment of splashing and then the periods of silence becoming longer. Marlan never cried out again.

I tried to wrench away from Ali. "We can't stand by and let him drown," I shouted. But Ali's grip only tightened and I found myself unable to move. His face was as placid as though he were listening to far off music. He didn't answer me. He caught my other arm as I lifted it for the blow. After a moment, when I knew it was hopeless, I stopped struggling.

As we stood quietly on the edge of the pool, Marlan drowned.

After a bit the water ceased to throw off agitated diamond light and slowly became another dark sky with the moon and the stars held rigid once more in mirror-like reflection. The white swan became still. I remembered the beautiful woman with the flowing blond hair and wondered whether soon she would return to ride once again astride the swan amid the sound of laughter and ice tinkling in shakers. All about us lay the deserted trappings of Marlan's world with the owner drowned at the bottom of his own marble pool. For a long time neither of us said a word.

Ali was the first to speak. "Come with me," he said gently.

Wearily I stooped to retrieve the torn burnoose and followed him away from the pool.

"You've been following me all along," I said.

"Not I. But someone told me where to find you."

He stopped abruptly and I drew up beside him. Down on the main road the lights of three cars were heading swiftly towards the entrance to the gates.

"It is the police. They have come for Marlan's body. They know, of course, he has committed suicide."

"How could they have *known*?"

"If it had not been that way it would have been another. Come. It is wiser that we do not have conversation with the police."

He seemed very calm and sure of himself. Without undue haste he led the way around the summer house, down through the formal gardens behind the main house and finally out onto a wide plain covered with scrublike underbrush. Majestically he led me out across the plain.

Suddenly I saw the plane flying low overhead, a plane which was obviously rising from a take-off.

"Pinel?" I asked.

"It is probably so."

"And Madame Fayne and the boy?"

Ali shrugged.

"Well, there goes my last way out," I said.

Instead of answering, Ali stooped low, pushed aside some heavy underbrush, and we stepped out into a narrow road, no more than tire tracks across the plain.

"You are a pessimist," he said, as he straightened up. He looked at me and smiled. I couldn't blame him much. I didn't cut an heroic figure in my underclothes and a torn burnoose over my arm.

Up ahead a shadow resolved into the old Buick touring car in which Ali had made his dramatic appearance earlier this evening, with an Arab at the wheel. Ali stepped aside and motioned me in. In a moment, we were lumbering, without benefit of lights, across the plain.

"Why are you doing this, Ali?"

"There are many reasons. I believe most of them are good."

I knew there was no use in further questions. The car left the plains and when we struck a main road the driver switched on the lights. We began to make better time. Soon we turned into a private driveway, went speeding past a house which was a more modest edition of Marlan's palace and came to a halt on the edge of a small, private airdrome. A smart looking amphibian was warming up in preparation for a take-off.

"What's this?" I asked Ali.

"It was once the private plane of Mr. Marlan. I am sure he would be delighted to know that his pilot has taken it on himself to take you and Mrs. Fayne from the country."

"Mrs. Fayne! Then Pinel did not take her with him?"

"No, his mission is complete. There was no need to bring Mrs. Fayne to trial. She preferred to wait behind for you."

We started across the field towards the plane. Someone came forward and handed me an overcoat but I was hardly aware of it. Automatically I put it on.

"You will find your clothes in the plane," Ali said.

Claire stood in the door of the plane's cabin waiting for me. The look of relief on her face told me all I needed to know.

I said to Ali, "It will take her a long time to forget tonight. After all, she killed a man—"

"It was an act of war," Ali said simply.

"Even then..."

"And there is the young effendi, Mr. Denby. It is his world that will count. The world of all our sons."

"Yes," I said, "Some day I hope Charles can look back on Marlan's world as only a dim nightmare from his youth."

"That is the hope of us all."

When we were almost at the plane he reached into his robes, drew something forth and handed it to me. He was smiling again. "Perhaps," he said with the merest trace of irony in his voice, "This will bring you luck, Mr. Denby. It is useless to us. M. Pinel and your friends were mistaken. We helped you because we knew you to be good. But we stopped using this as a means of identification many months ago. However, it is a nice souvenir."

"Thanks," I said dryly, "I'll give it to Charles as a play-thing."

I moved then towards Claire holding the object in my hand which was, of course, the Persian Cat.

THE END

John Gearon, better known to readers as John Flagg, was born in 1885 in Chicago, Illinois, and educated in Englewood, New Jersey. Leaving school in his senior year, he travelled throughout Europe and the Near East. He became a radio script writer for the Office of the Coordinator for Inter-American Affairs, later working in a literary agency and as a journalist. With Louis Bromfield, Gearon co-wrote a Broadway play set in Paris in 1935. He published his first novel, *The Velvet Well*, in 1946—filmed by Jacques Deray in 1978 as *A Butterfly on the Shoulder*—followed by a series of thrillers for Gold Medal Books in the 1950s under the name John Flagg. These include six books featuring post-war agent, Hart Muldoon. Gearon died in 1970.